We Are All Equally Far from Love

We Are All
Equally Far from Love
by Adania Shibli

translated from the Arabic
by Paul Starkey

clockroot books

First published in the United States in 2012 by

Clockroot Books
An imprint of Interlink Publishing Group, Inc.
46 Crosby Street
Northampton, Massachusetts 01060
www.clockrootbooks.com
www.interlinkbooks.com

Originally published in Arabic as *Kulluna Ba'id bi-Dhat al-Miqdar 'an al-Hubb* by al-Adab in 2004

Library of Congress Cataloging-in-Publication Data

Shibli, 'Adaniyah.
[Kulluna ba'id bi-dhat al-miqdar 'an al-hubb. English]
We are all equally far from love / by Adania Shibli ; translated by
Paul Starkey. -- 1st American ed.
p. cm.
ISBN 978-1-56656-863-0 (pbk.)
I. Starkey, Paul. II. Title.
PJ7962.H425K7513 2011
808.83--dc23
2011033314

Printed and bound in the United States of America

Contents

The Beginning

Yesterday, while it was still fine and hadn't yet started to rain, I went with the neighbors' children to a local park to play. The four of us ran around, hiding here and there, and there were lots of butterflies that looked as if they were playing with us. Afterwards we sat on a large rock, and it was then that I discovered I was seeing everything in order to write about it to him. More than that, I discovered that I had forgotten how to live without his letters. It made me afraid of finding myself one day without them.

A few hours later, when I arrived home, I found a short letter from him.

We had been exchanging letters for two years.

I'd written him my first letter at the suggestion of my boss, to ask his opinion on something, as he didn't like talking directly to strangers. I composed my words carefully, and a little fearfully.

Two days later he replied cursorily, and perhaps with a touch of warmth. I could detect this warmth between the words, and it made me happy for the whole of the afternoon, for no particular reason except most likely that I was a weak person who was touched by hints like this, and quite easily.

The next letter I sent to him went out a month later, asking him again for his opinion on the same matter, for I hadn't completely understood what he'd told me the first time. He replied. His second letter was also short. Both his letters to me were shorter than mine to him, and he also concluded them more abruptly than I did. He wished me "Best," while I closed my letters with "Best wishes." I don't know why I offered more right from the beginning.

Then the days once more started to pass as they had before, uselessly. I wasn't happy with my work, nor with anything else. I was living mechanically, doing everything with a sort of lifeless proficiency, though the presence of his two letters in a file on the shelf in my office forced me, illogically and inexplicably, to go to work each day. His two letters, plus a walnut tree whose branches hung over a house wall and across the sidewalk where I walked to get to work. Every day I would pass under those branches. I could have crossed to the opposite sidewalk, but I had become addicted to the sense of pride that flooded through me when I had to lower my head to pass under the tree, especially in winter when its slender, leafless branches became more fragile. At the end of spring, the branches would start to fill with leaves, forcing me to stoop lower, while in fall, those same leaves would race me as I walked on, until they would suddenly stop, or blow away in a different direction.

His two letters had a similar effect. Like the tree, they were able to touch me and my loneliness, and the kindness that emanated from them did not disappear with time. I even found myself wishing that I could think of a new subject to give me an excuse to write him a third letter.

But everything in my life was monotonous.

I wrote him a third letter.

I told him that I had quit my job and moved to live somewhere else. Here was my new address. I wrote a number of similar letters, which I sent to some acquaintances, to lessen the sense of stupidity and the alienation that I felt from myself. I hesitated for a long, long time before sending him the letter.

He didn't reply.

Some weeks later, a friend pointed out to me that there was a mistake in the address I had sent him. I felt utterly stupid again, but this time it was stupidity of a different kind. I corrected the address then re-sent it to everybody, but not to him. Better not to.

Perhaps what had drawn me to him from the beginning was the beginning itself, when my boss asked me to write someone a letter instead of speaking to him on the telephone, as if the person in question found great satisfaction in isolating himself. No, he didn't want to talk to anyone, and there was not a single hope in the world that would lure him. The shortness of his two letters to me suggested that he didn't even regret this isolation. I, on the other hand, had never been able to say "no" in my life; I was always full of illogical hopes. Perhaps my desire for him was one of these hopes.

A few days later I sent him the correct address.

Had he not replied?

4

Then I dissolved in a sort of feeling of contempt for myself, and tried to forget him as much as I could.

The new house that I'd recently moved to had hastened the stages of my withdrawal from living and other people's troubles. The new job was just like nothing, or worse, for even lunch during the midday break had lost its flavor. Then, as time went on, the kitchen tap started to drip, until eventually it no longer bothered me.

After that, the rain started, and I would remember the walnut tree, and how the drops of rain would stay there suspended on its branches even after the weather had brightened. I would walk under the tree and sometimes bang against a branch, which would shake so that raindrops fell from it. How nice that was.

It was still raining outside when I heard the garden gate move, and my elderly neighbor came in. She started to deal with the drain, removing the dry leaves that had collected on top of it. "Why don't you write to him again?" I said to myself. "You reached a high point of stupidity

5

the last time, so a fourth letter can't do much harm."

But he replied. He talked about the cold, and how bitter it was. That he didn't like the town I lived in, and wasn't particularly interested in trees. Finally, to solve the problem of the tap, an ancient Greek philosopher had advised wrapping a cotton thread around the spout, so that the drops of water would flow gently down the thread and disappear into the drain.

From that day on, the letters between us never stopped. At first, they appeared an average of once a month, then gradually this became once a week.

My letters to him at first began "Dear Sir," and continued with "Dear Sir," until suddenly these two words acquired resonances and connotations that I felt I needed to be wary of, so I persuaded myself that they were not there.

Despite this, it was only when I was writing to him and reading his letters that I would feel myself. For although I had never in my life heard his voice, never seen him, never touched him, he aroused in me something that stirred the desire for life.

I started trying to find other meanings and hidden worlds in the words he had written. If he ended a letter with "Love," I would find myself searching for all the connotations and allusions that this word might have, using the dictionary as a neutral and reliable source of information.

Then I would think things over and try to persuade myself to calm down. But to no avail. He pursued me like a breeze behind my neck. I could feel him quite close to me, even on the narrow path leading to my house. I could feel him every morning, when I heard the sound of my elderly neighbor, at first behind the bedroom window, then later behind the kitchen window as she shut the door behind her and walked over the stones of the garden path, followed by the slow crinkling of a plastic bag.

How much he wasn't here!

But we were writing. He was perhaps the only person that I felt was able to see and completely understand the sort of life that I found myself living, where the three most important things to me were a walnut tree, watching the movements of my elderly neighbor, and waiting for his letters.

He would send me a letter that reached me every Sunday morning, while for my part I would write to him every day. Still I would wait until Wednesday before sending him everything I'd written, for I was afraid that he would become bored and desert me if I sent him a letter every day. This fear made me sad, but I gave in to it nonetheless.

But I didn't admit that I was in love with him until that short letter reached me yesterday, asking me to put an end to our correspondence and not to send him any more letters.

The tears leaped to my eyes. I would have liked to tell him no. I should have, but instead I sat and wrote "I love you," and then everything.

That was the first letter. He didn't reply. The pain was intense, but I paid no attention, and wrote the second letter. Again, he didn't reply. The pain became more intense, so I wrote a third letter, and felt at peace. I wrote without needing to wait for Wednesday, three days were enough. I wrote a fourth letter, then a fifth, willing myself not to write any more.

I think about him all day long. What's my mistake? That I love him? That I've started to love him?

That I've told him I love him? That I don't know him at all?

    I am tired. Even the noise of the plastic bag between my neighbor's fingers has begun to hurt me.

But I wrote to him again. I no longer cared about anything. Everything was heading towards death, with nothing to stop it.

The First Measure

As if every beginning is an end

She left school today. After she had repeated fourth grade twice, seventh grade twice, and was this year about to repeat ninth grade as well, her father raised his eyebrows and said no. This was precisely the movement that Afaf had been waiting for since fourth grade, but her father's laziness had delayed it all those years.

Despite the fact that her grandfather had been a revolutionary, and been killed in 1948, her father was a collaborator. The government had entrusted him with a variety of tasks for various ministries, such as the receipt of requests for issuing identity cards, travel permits, building permits, postal services, approval of telephone line connections, permits to sell diesel, and so on. But because he had accumulated excess fat in every corner of his body, and was therefore rather overweight—as well as having a thick moustache, and a large gold ring on the finger of his right hand—he had distributed most of the spying tasks among the members of his family. He himself had only the task of operating the small recorder that sat in the pocket of his always clean and ironed white shirt. He was a lazy man, and he seldom stirred from his place under the almond tree. But then again, he had no need to do so, not even to leave his seat, to know what conspiracies the locals were hatching up that might jeopardize state security. The locals would come to him themselves, and being so lazy and obese, if he could, he would have called her to press the button on the recorder in his shirt pocket.

Afaf crossed the square to go back home, leaving her father where he sat in the shade under the tree. She felt that the sun, which had blazed above her through the final days of the school year, was now determined to melt her. The two circles of sweat visible on her school shirt under her arms were spreading like wildfire.

She went up the steps into the house, breathing a sigh of relief when she found them clean, a sign that her father's wife had finished the housework. She went inside, and went into the room she shared with her siblings.

Sitting down on the bed, she ran her hands over her face to wipe the sweat away, then took a long breath, as if to say "Thank God." She turned her hands over again in front of her eyes, which twinkled despite the lack of light in the room. Little by little she started to return to her senses from the giddiness caused by the heat of the sun.

It was only then that she realized how heavy the bag on her back had been. She took it off, and put it down on the ground for the last time.

From now on it would be a handbag. Goodbye, back!

She stood up to take off her school clothes, then headed towards the sewing machine in the sitting room and took out a pair of scissors from under the cover. Her father's wife of course jumped out to ask her what the scissors were for, but she didn't reply. This creature didn't seem to understand that she didn't want to talk to her, ever. Then she cut her school trousers, thereby announcing the severing of all ties with the educational system and emphasizing the impossibility of returning to it. She cut them up to the knee, so that no one would open their mouth, though they would anyway, but it was her father that really mattered. She ate her father's wife's bland food then went out. And she heard her; every letter of the word rang in her ears: "Slut."

Expressions like this only served to emphasize that it was she, her father's wife, who was the slut, but there was no justice in this world. She didn't want to go back to fight with her, and spoil her mood and the happiness she felt that school had totally disappeared from her world. She crossed the square and headed towards the almond tree, where her father was sitting, now staring at her legs from a distance. As she reached him, his voice emerged from under his moustache with difficulty.

"What are these trousers?"

"Knee length," she replied indifferently.

"Oh, knee length," he repeated. Then, after perhaps a couple of seconds: "You really are your mother's daughter!"

"Or maybe my father's," she found herself answering.

Then his house shoe was flying straight through the air towards her head. As it struck her, for a few seconds all she could feel was the place where it had hit.

"You slut!" he continued.

She retraced her steps with her father's shoe still ringing in her head, then his orders followed: "Tomorrow you'll get up early and open the post office. Don't think that just because you've quit school you can laze around in bed until noon."

One day, one day God willing, she'd shoot him and his wife with the same revolver that he kept behind his back. She wouldn't take off her trousers, even over her dead body, and then let him open the post office himself every day.

She came in and had a wash, then quickly cleaned the bathroom. There was nothing for her to worry about today, or tomorrow either. She stood in front of the mirror combing her hair and redoing her calculations. Alright, so let it be the post, at least she'd finally been saved from school and housework.

Her only remaining problem in life was that her hair was frizzy. From her box, originally a chocolate box, which she had taken with her to the bathroom, she took out a dozen black hairpins that her mother had left behind with some other things, removed them all from the piece of cardboard they had been attached to for several years, and laid them out in front of her. For a moment, the darkness around her was filled with a soft, gentle clinking as the pins bounced off one another and off the edge of the mirror where she had spilled them. The time had come to start paying some attention to herself, now that she was no longer a school girl: shape her eyebrows, for example, put on some kohl, and straighten her hair.

She combed her hair again, parting it on the left, and started to push the pins into it, wrapping the hair round her head from left to right, and spacing the pins three fingers apart. When she had finished she covered it with a kerchief, then went back to the bedroom, laid her head on the pillow and went to sleep.

As she was fast asleep, enjoying an afternoon snooze, the pillow underneath her was slowly and insistently getting soaked by her wet hair and the sweat pouring from her face with the heat of the day. Her sweating was made even worse by the horrid dreams that the hurtful words of her father and his wife had given her.

After a couple of hours or so she woke up for a few moments, but stayed in bed, her head feeling heavy and numb. Only the voices of some soap opera characters filled the emptiness of the house. Then she went back to sleep again until the morning.

In the morning, she undid her kerchief, and to her great delight found her hair smooth, so that she seemed almost pretty. She rewrapped her hair again with the kerchief, though, for she didn't want to waste her beauty. She poured herself a glass of tea, which she drank standing in front of the kitchen sink, while her siblings sat behind her eating their breakfast, with her father's wife beside them, polluting the air with her foul breath and foul words. When she had finished she put the empty glass in the sink, took the keys to the post office from the hook and went out.

As soon as she opened the door, she was hit by a cold breeze that made a shiver go up her arms. Gradually, for the millionth time, the light slipping through the open door behind her revealed the contents of the office. But as from now on she would be working among them and beside them every day, this time she looked at the room's contents slowly and in a different way.

On the wall to her right hung an old white fan, under which was a large board showing the various postal charges in great detail by weight and destination. There was no need to read it to the end, however: the first line on the left was more than enough, for all that the local people ever mailed were letters weighing less than

25 grams to addresses inside the country. It was true that, very occasionally, hobbies like pen pal correspondence, horseback riding, or swimming would become fashionable, but because there were only a few horses, and swimming pools didn't exist, that left only the possibility of pen pal correspondence. So a person would send no more than one or two letters abroad in his whole life—between ninth and twelfth grade, to be precise, by which time, after several years of studying the language, a few people were finally able to write a letter in English.

Lost souls, all looking for a rich old lady from Europe or America to adopt them, and save them from a life back home that would be a mere extension of the monotonous school uniform. All these dreams... if it hadn't been for these dreams, students would never have done any of their geography or English homework.

Then all would collapse with a hint from their families, as it became clear how unrealistic these sorts of dreams were. So they would give up their pen pal hobby and move on to the second dream: work, and how to get together a tenth of what it might cost to build or buy a house. The full sum would be made up through the generosity of grandfathers and grandmothers, offering what they had saved from their national insurance allowance, and what they had hidden under the floor, and with the help of mothers, fathers, brothers and sisters. When it came to the stage of laying the floor, the new house owner would take to standing in the square on the lookout for a serious girl who didn't laugh, didn't turn left or right like a horse in blinders, and who hadn't been around when he wrote those words of his several years before on the pages of notebooks in the space that lay opposite the word "hobby." And so together, hand in hand, he and his prey would begin their endless journey into boredom, whose carefully planned path did not include the need for the means of communication represented by the postal service, the operation of which would from today on rest on Afaf's shoulders.

To the left, beside the wall, stood a large purple plastic bucket that served as a waste bin, above which hung a gray public telephone, while in the middle of the room stood a long dark-colored wooden counter. This counter was effectively the "post office." On it had been placed a few items of essential equipment: a pen, the end of which was attached to a long piece of string fastened to the inside of the counter with a nail; and a small container made from a hollow piece of wood and full of water, inside which was a wide cylindrical device used for sticking on the stamps, though Afaf would not use it, preferring to use her own saliva.

The inside of the counter concealed another world. There was a second shelf, with a "spying" notebook, a receipt book, and a folder of stamps, all hidden from the eyes of those sending letters. Behind the shelf was a chair that could revolve and crawl in all directions.

Then finally, at the rear of the office there was a large wall clock, with a small sentence in the middle indicating that it was a gift from a well-known insurance company, while to the left of the clock hung a torn and dirty flag. Under this there was a picture of the Head of State, which was not as dirty as the flag, as democracy forced them to change it from time to time.

Afaf drew up the chair and sat down in anticipation of a dearth of callers. After a while, she lifted her hand to her hair and began to feel the loose pins, fixing them in place again. At that moment, she recalled her mother, and how she would open a pin between her teeth with the help of her left hand while her right hand clasped a lock of hair.

By the time it was almost ten, Afaf had finished thinking about everything. She still had about twenty minutes of complete boredom in front of her before she could regain a bit of life as the letters arrived. But the heat did not help her. The blasts of hot air coming in through the open door from outside made the time stretch out even longer than usual, making her feel even more bored. She hit the table hard with her hand, then quickly withdrew it with a cry. She hadn't expected it to hurt that much.

Afaf's main task in the post office was to open and read the letters, then inform her father of the contents. A certain person originally from the quarter who now lived in America also sometimes sent letters addressed to his family in "Palestine," which she had to erase and replace with "Israel." It was quite normal for the locals' letters to arrive opened. If a letter arrived unopened, they explained it as being due to the existence of a stick of glue in the post office, which would soon run out. A new development with Afaf 's entry into the office, however, was the arguments that broke out between her and the young men and women of the quarter, who complained that their letters were arriving with certain sections deleted. The prevailing belief was that the sentences deleted contained a reference to an enclosure with the letter, a gift from the sender that Afaf had decided to confiscate after it had taken her fancy. Some people went as far as to complain about her to her father, who replied from behind his moustache under the almond tree: "That's life!" But in Afax presence his couldn't-care-less attitude turned into the roar of a large and angry animal.

But in vain!

Another new development after she took over was the appearance, for the first time since the postal authority had entered the locality, of inscriptions on the wooden counter, carved by her bored hand with the help of the post office key. These included the following: "Afaf"; a dagger with three drops of blood dripping from it; 9/8/71, her date of birth; 9/13/81, her "mother's date"; 6/31/87, the date she had quit school; and a heart pierced by an arrow that began at a point starting with the letter A and ended with a question mark.

This question mark suggested only one possible answer, namely that she was not destined for a love story. On the other hand, she would certainly marry, for her father wielded great authority, and this would doubtless sooner or later extend to finding a groom for her from somewhere, even if they had to dig one up. Most likely it would be sometime between sooner and later, that is, before she became an old maid, but after he had exploited her a little for the post office service.

Afaf began to imagine married life, together with the housework—which she was currently spared—that would again fall on her shoulders as a result. Perhaps she would be happy. But that was impossible. Her whole life was a heap of shit, and her luck certainly wasn't going to change and bring her happiness. What on earth could possibly change? A strange husband certainly wouldn't have any more love or affection for her than her own parents!

Suddenly she heard the sound of a dove flapping its wings. It had apparently been standing at the door of the post office. For a few moments the dove lifted her from her gloomy thoughts, and she wondered what it could be doing in a dark, arid place like this. Then she sighed.

This was the first time Afaf had ever sighed properly. She felt a little more mature, and started to reflect on what had happened. Her breath had come out, and she felt that a weight had been lifted from her chest. That is why people sigh, then. That is what had finally, and quite naturally, happened to her. When she was younger, she had tried hard to sigh to imitate her mother, for she loved the tone and rhythm of her mother's frequent sighs.

Alone in the office, far from the world, she felt quite safe recalling her mother. Sometimes, she would even find herself longing for her, despite everything that her mother had done.

Afaf didn't know where her mother was now or what she was doing. She didn't know how or why everything had happened. One day, in the fourth grade, just a few days after the start of the first term, she and her siblings had woken up to find that their usual tea and breakfast wasn't ready. She looked for her mother in her parents' bedroom, but found it empty. She went all around the house but couldn't find her. However much time she spent searching in it, it was completely useless. Perhaps she was in the vegetable garden. Her mother sometimes went there, so she decided to go to look for her there. As she went out, she found her aunt on the steps, and before she could open her mouth, her aunt said scornfully: "Not a word! Give your siblings their breakfast, then all of you go to school."

At noon that day, 9/13/1981, as she and her siblings sat round the table to have lunch, their father announced from behind his moustache that it was henceforth forbidden for any of them to mention the word "mummy" or to ask about her. His right hand was clasping his revolver as he said it, while his left hand was empty except for some lines cast by the light from the kitchen window. The facts that emerged as Afaf secretly collected scraps from other people's gossip were to make that day the longest day of her life. In fact, they extended so far as to take over her entire life, changing it into an endless scandal, a heap of dirt that never stopped growing: her mother had run off with another man.

Afaf clasped her hands together and ran the backs of her hands over the pins in her hair. At the same time, she gave a quick look at the clock on the wall behind her, which once again said ten past ten.

More than three months had passed since Afaf started work in the post office. Her sufferings had neither increased nor decreased, as she had completely surrendered to her fate after the first occasion, even before she had finished turning the key to open the office door for the second time. Most letters contained nothing that could possibly threaten state security, or even any exciting news to amuse her, until suddenly *those* letters arrived.

Six letters that did not bear the name or even the address of the sender, written by a woman to a local man who had been living in Italy for a number of years but had returned home just a month and a half ago. With her secret service mentality, Afaf guessed that the letters had originally been sent to Italy, then sent back again to him here. In fact, there had been a number of letters sent to him by this route, which is what aroused her suspicions about him in the first place. The important thing, however, was that, though the woman's letters did not contain any gifts or valuables, Afaf found them highly interesting, and this led her to confiscate them, one after the other.

She read and reread them dozens of times, so often that she surprised herself with her ability to learn things by heart, something that both she and her Arabic teacher had given up hope of. She hadn't even been able to memorize the line of poetry that talks about "Rebab, the cock and the oil."

It wasn't just that these letters were love letters, they also opened the door to a profitable scheme, for the local girls quickly picked up the news that Afaf had love letters for sale, and anyone lacking talent or the ability to write started drawing on them for inspiration. Thus, the letters acquired an even wider circulation than the beauty products that the "Emperor of Gaza," one of the best-known traveling salesmen in the region, tried to sell. The letters may even have reached their original target via another girl who had fallen in love with the reticent man now back from Italy.

As time went on, Afaf started to wait for those letters impatiently. When they arrived, she was even happier than when a present turned up in a letter, even if it was a ring or a necklace. But nothing had come from the woman for more than two weeks. There were only the six letters, with their lines of writing almost illegible at the folds, after Afaf had opened and closed them so many times. And now they were all cramped in the same box with the hairpins, bringing neither profit nor love to anyone.

The Second Measure

As if every beginning is an end,
Just as we begin, an ending comes

She had forgotten to cut the chicken up. She had put it into the pot whole, and now the pot had begun to boil so it was too late to take it out. She went leaping around the kitchen, hitting and hating herself.

She looked around her slowly and carefully, trying to find another mistake that she might have committed while she was daydreaming about him. She had put the vegetables into the pot that she needed for rice, though that was a tolerable mistake.

She drew up the chair and sat down, her eyes fixed on the guilty pot, while the flame underneath it burned on insistently and carelessly. At least there was no one else in the house.

She got up again to fetch a cigarette to smoke in the kitchen. She would try to stop smoking.

From time to time the sound of the chicken boiling away on the flame was joined by the hum of the refrigerator. She gazed at the ring that had sat on the finger of her left hand for so long that the flesh had swollen up around it.

It was incomprehensible how she no longer loved him. What a long time ago that was. She felt as if she had been released from a torment whose details she had now forgotten. All those evening lectures that he would give her, before he fell asleep and she burst into tears. He had treated her badly enough for her to feel no guilt when she fell in love with another man; just pity, nothing more. Even his appearance had changed. He had become darker. He had become thinner too, and had changed his hairstyle, which made him look even more stupid.

It was good for his health for him to be loved.

She couldn't believe that after loving him for all those years, she had fallen in love again with a man, thereby blotting her husband completely out of her life except for a single meal when he returned from work, and his presence in the left-hand side of the bed.

Three months ago she had experienced a spasm in her left shoulder. It was this shoulder that had been closer to her husband and his evil, when one night he endlessly and mercilessly abused her.

She'd been sure it wouldn't provoke him when she asked him if he'd object to not breaking into the savings account they had opened to provide for the children's university education in the future. Current circumstances did not inspire confidence, and it would perhaps be better for them instead to take a loan from the bank. He wanted to buy a new car, as he was fed up with taking it to the garage every weekend.

She could no longer move it, her shoulder, that is, after that night's conversation.

The doctor, who was completely unfamiliar with the bitter chain of events in her life, had said that it was the result of a sudden nervous shock, and advised her to book some physiotherapy sessions immediately.

She drove to the first session herself, with one hand, because her husband was first of all busy, and secondly didn't believe her. She lay down on the narrow white couch with her eyes closed, waiting for the session to begin.

When had the love started?

Right at the beginning, when he asked her, "Did I hurt you?"

That was like an ancient question that no longer crossed the mind of anyone she knew. If he *had* hurt her, the question would have wiped out any trace of any pain, past or future. But the answer stuck in her throat, and all she did was make a sort of sobbing sound that sounded like a no. He asked her again and this time she tried her best to say "no!" properly. She raised her head, her spasms got worse, and a faint moan escaped her lips. He apologized, and she asked him not to.

From the beginning, then, it seemed that the treatment was not just aimed at her stiff shoulder, but at her broken heart. The thing she'd believed was the worst thing to happen in her entire life began to change—how, she didn't know—into something beautiful that brought back her sense of her humanity. After this she no longer had any choice but to love him.

Then they started to talk about the Phoenicians in the North and other people in the East.

She liked anything to do with ancient civilizations and the birth of the monotheistic religions.

Subjects like these suited the lifestyle of a woman in her forties, a frustrated woman who spent all day working outside the house and all night working inside it. They were subjects that went into and out of her life without changing anything of importance in the routine she had been living for fifteen years. She was embarrassed to reveal these interests to anyone, though. Certainly not to her husband, who didn't even hear when she asked him if he would like a coffee. And her children lived with quite enough fear and tension from their homework assignments.

So when she couldn't find anything to say to the man whose hand was passing over her, and suddenly started to recall that her husband had hardly touched her all those years, even when they were starting their feeble lovemaking, she ventured to talk to him about the Phoenicians. And he responded by talking about the Assyrians.

When he asked her whether she knew King Solomon, she responded by asking, "Personally?" and he burst out laughing.

This was the first time she had heard him laugh. She had tried to imagine him laughing during the last few days but she hadn't imagined him laughing as he was now. The laughter burst straight into her ears and touched her deeply. And then a smile spread over her face as well, without her intending it.

She didn't laugh with her husband, and her husband didn't laugh with her. When he laughed, he laughed *at* her, to make fun of her. His laughter would make her shoulder ache and bring tears and a choking feeling to her throat.

When he made her once again discover that she didn't understand anything, her stomach would turn. She needed him—or rather, she had come to need him—to be certain that even her feelings were true. Then as time went on it wasn't just her opinions that were wrong, it was her questions too. So, when he asked her whether she knew King Solomon and she replied "Personally?" it was a serious question.

But luckily he laughed.

She hurried out to the car and drove home as fast as possible to read what the Song of Songs and the Book of Ecclesiastes had to say on the matter, as if King Solomon had finished the two manuscripts and the two books emerged from typesetting and printing just now rather than three thousand years ago.

Three thousand years since the king had fallen in love with the shepherdess. Three thousand years since her heart had been moved with the same sort of desire: to hurry home, her heart behind the steering wheel almost running, as it ordered all the traffic lights to change to green immediately.

"There is nothing new under the sun," said the King. But for her, the sun itself was new. To love, to go to sleep and wake up again, and still be in love. To bathe and love, to cook and love. To drive the car and love, and to love the sun.

The routine of her life was not ready, however, to absorb all this energy. She had to pour it into a small project set up behind the house. Three small garden beds in which she sowed mint, parsley, and basil.

As time went on, these three small beds let her distance herself from the life she had been leading for years. Finally, she was able to be with herself, as she had been once, before turning into a wife and then a mother. She could touch the earth, and water the beds. When the weather was warm and the sun straight above her, drops of sweat would gather on her nose. Then she would go to rest in the shade and recall how he had run his hand over her time and again.

It was her husband who got the first sprig of mint, which swam in front of him in a cup of tea. They had both forgotten his previous great sarcasm with regard to her agricultural project, when he accused her of yet another pretentious obsession. So how could she not give him the first sprig of mint?

She was sitting on his left in the sitting room, both of them smoking, while he talked. Everything he said was rubbish, and boring, but she would nod her head from time to time in agreement. Suddenly he looked directly at her, and in a tone both mocking and threatening said: "You've become stronger!"

She responded with a smile, and he added, "You will pay the price for this strength."

He left the sitting room, and she remained sitting to the left of nothing, thinking about this man to whom she'd spent the whole of her life giving love, absolute love. She wouldn't let the tears steal from her eyes, still fixed on a door that had just been quietly closed.

She sat down to write him a letter.

She picked up a pair of scissors and began by trimming the uneven edges on the right side of the page that she had ripped from her daughter's Arabic exercise book, then started to look for a pen with a fine nib, not too broad.

After several hours, made up of five minutes here and five minutes there, granted to her, probably unintentionally, by a world crowded with cares and demands, the letter was ready, together with the last treatment session. A letter in which she had decided she should finally be herself, even though she was profoundly afraid that she might appear very stupid.

She folded it twice, extra carefully, so that each fold contained the same number of lines. Then, intentionally this time, she hid it under her husband's socks. Usually, he didn't bother to look any further than the socks he would be wearing. If his natural field of vision nonetheless forced him to take in a white piece of paper, he wouldn't bother to open it, and if he did open it and saw her handwriting, he would never bother to read it.

For the first time in her life she was taking some pleasure in his couldn't-care-less attitude and lack of concern for her; and she was even flirting with it.

"I never believed that writing would be harder than talking. Can you imagine? Anyway, I love you.

Perhaps you will be thinking what brought me into your path. Isn't life difficult enough without all this? But that's what basically happened to me. This is not any sort of declaration of war, or anything like that, but simply a declaration of all that is sweet and kind, and of what makes life worth living.

You must be nervous now. Anyway, life is very short. Why don't we live it day by day, enjoying the beauty of existence whenever we can. I have never believed that conventions are more powerful than feelings.

So I cannot stop myself from imagining us together. This time, I will hold you very close, press my hands on your body, and feel you breathe.

Please don't be angry at me for writing words like these, or thinking them. Just read them."

He told her that she shouldn't feel that way about him.

She left his office, and as she had no strength for anything else, she started to walk. She walked past her own car, then past some other cars, until she had left the entire parking lot behind her. She hid herself away behind some buildings in an out-of-the-way square, found a wooden bench seat and sat down on it. She looked at her neat black clothes and the gold necklace around her neck. Some woolen threads had caught in the necklace as it dangled over her sweater, so she carefully removed them. Then she went on, thinking of what to cook today, though she knew that that was merely rubbish with which she was trying to distract herself.

The Third Measure

As if every beginning is an end,
Just as we begin, an ending comes,
Suddenly, its touch unfelt

Suddenly, now, on his way to work at half past nine in the morning, his eyes filled with tears. He could no longer bear it.

The sorrow had begun to grow in his heart, stifling his faltering breath. He raised his head to breathe and to stop the flow of his tears.

He had been recalling it since morning. A dream that was so real it had got the better of him when he woke and discovered that it was just a dream. He couldn't believe that a dream could be so like reality, or that reality could be so straightforward. He was going down the steps of an apartment block, with a girl beside him dressed in black. He had never seen her before. As she went with him down the stairs, a strong feeling of intimacy and trust arose between them. When they reached the ground floor, they saw an ice cream truck parked outside, and the girl turned to him and asked him to buy her an ice cream. So they walked the rest of the way to the truck, her a few paces in front, happy because he was about to treat her. When they reached the truck's window, she leaned on the sill to see what flavors there were and make her choice, while he stayed behind her, looking at her and at her feet, which had started to lift off the ground in her enthusiasm. At that point he noticed that her underwear, the outline of which could be clearly seen through her pants, had slipped down towards her crotch. He slipped his fingers over her crotch and was casually starting to explore it, when he suddenly woke up.

The sky to which he had just lifted his eyes was very blue, perhaps because of the strong wind that wouldn't let any cloud stay there for more than a couple of minutes. God, if only he hadn't woken up!

The sky was blue, then. Perhaps it was good that it was blue and that he was looking at it. At least he wasn't staring at anyone. He looked like a fool, the way he stared at people, as if he were somehow seeking something from them.

The wind picked up again, carrying to him the sound of the three flags that fluttered in the distance, where they flew in front of the municipal building. The sight reminded him that he was still there and that he shouldn't loiter any longer. No sooner had he recollected himself and lowered his gaze from the sky, when, at that very moment, from behind the coating of tears that were about to dry up, he saw her.

She was sitting on the only wooden bench in the square, dressed in black.

Black.

All sorts of thoughts rushed into his head as he hurried past the steel bars that separated the square from the parking lot opposite it. He knew the stones of this hateful square one by one. He had walked over them at least four times a day, six times a week for more than seven months, and apart from council employees in the sanitation department—garbage collectors, that is—during their lunch breaks, he had never seen anyone there, so who was this woman?

It couldn't just be coincidence that she was wearing black. It must be some sort of sign, especially as she was the first thing he had seen after lowering his eyes from the sky. But was it possible that there should still be some hope for him? No.

But why not?

No, none of it was credible. Why was he indulging in such hopes and fantasies? It was impossible that anything should happen between them. It was only a short distance. He looked at the square, trying to measure it. Fifty stone squares? About fifteen meters? And he dreamed of a woman every day. True, not as clearly as last night, but every day there was a woman. In addition, many people wore black, especially at this time of year.

The wind died down around him, to be replaced by a gentle breeze, perhaps because of the small building that he was just starting to pass. At that moment two birds passed in front of him, winging their way to a small pool of stagnant water left in the square by a faulty water meter. As the birds started bathing, he found himself staring again at the face of the woman, who was now just fourteen meters away. He had already acknowledged to himself that she was not at all like the woman of his dream. Nor was she pretty. She was a bit fat, and gave the impression of having lost her looks. She was also quite old, and the shape of her sagging breasts could be clearly made out underneath her sweater. But still, he wouldn't be much of a catch either.

After a few minutes, however, he changed his mind, and came to the conclusion that her face resembled, or maybe it just reminded him of, Leila's face. Leila was a doll that his uncle had brought him from Frankfurt airport, an enormous place that one could easily get lost in. He didn't know what had come over his uncle to single him out from all his fifty nephews and nieces to be presented with a doll, he really didn't know. It was a doll in the shape of a woman, who opened at the middle, then another woman appeared inside, who in turn opened in the middle to reveal another woman inside, and so on and so forth until a tiny woman appeared who did not open in the middle. He called this doll Leila.

Leila had stayed with him for years, so carefully guarded that he had not even allowed himself to play with her. He was apprehensive of anything that might harm her. Not one of his parents' early gentle attempts at persuasion had succeeded in getting him to give his brothers and sisters a chance to play with her. No, Leila was his and his alone. He was happy for her just to be there with him, hidden inside herself in his drawer.

This woman sitting in front of him, now at a distance of twelve meters, had the same way of looking as Leila, a look that refused to meet his

42

eyes. Ever since he had caught sight of her three meters before, with her face at a right angle to him, she had not turned at all. Her eyes had not moved either. He looked again at the pool of water to see what had happened to the two birds. He could not see them, but his eyes remained fixed on the small pool of water.

Until just a few moments ago he would have been pained by the sight of water being wasted while the whole region was suffering from drought. Had it not been for the faulty meter, however, which could be solved simply by changing the piece of plastic, those two birds would not have been able to take a bath or even to drink. His eyes began to follow the solitary pipe connecting the meter to the building. From the outside at least, the building appeared old and neglected, despite the still-visible evidence of previous repairs. In fact, it was a total wreck. There was a window blocked up with stones, for example, that looked extremely annoying. He couldn't understand why the person who had blocked it up hadn't properly finished the job. There were also remains of steps that no longer existed but had at one time led to the roof. He looked at her again. Ten meters until he would pass her. Could she have noticed him?

The wind was still blowing strongly around her. She was sitting in an exposed place, and her fine nose had turned a little red, perhaps because of the cold, or because of the lock of hair that had started to play naughty tricks above it. "*The wind and the air, how they play with her hair...*" Wasn't the breeze annoying her? "*The wind and the air...*" It was a nice song, even though he didn't like modern songs very much. He did like some of them, though; some of them were nice. Like Nawal al-Zughbi's song "*The nights have brought her back to me, brought back my heart's love to me!,*" for example. He used to like Ragheb 'Allama, but the Ragheb 'Allama of today wasn't like the old Ragheb 'Allama. He had yet to produce a better song than "The Sultan's Daughter." When he heard this song he could almost feel the water ripple. "*Oh daughter of the Sultan, have pity on your slave, the water's in your hands!*" The music would blare out from a small tape recorder inside their house, as his mother and sisters did the cleaning, and he waited on the balcony for them to finish, or at least until everything was dry. He would stay sitting out there with his feet up on the chair until they turned numb. Finally, after all the songs on the tape had finished, and after the parsley in the garden bed had almost wilted for lack of water, they would let him in. Then they would start shouting: "No, no, watch out, don't touch that! Don't leave any fingerprints on the cupboard! Be careful, don't tread on the carpet!" These memories stirred in him a longing for his family. He hadn't gone to see them for months. But a sudden loud noise of car horns turned his attention back to the square. She was still there in front of him, there on the wooden bench.

So far nothing had happened. In fact, nothing was going to happen. But goodness! How he longed to touch someone and feel the warmth of a human body in real life, not just in his dreams. To grasp her hand with his hand, the hand that still yearned for the warmth it had found one day inside some red underwear. How long would he have to keep going round and round to revive his memories of that time, when his father had taken him with him to visit some friends? At that time he had been crazy about high places, continually preoccupied with finding the highest place he could climb up to. People had started to build extra stories onto their buildings during that period, and despite the fact that these operations involved pouring wet concrete on top of the original walls, which made him extremely nervous, he liked the new sight of buildings being extended upwards. So it was quite natural that the house they had come to visit should be one of these buildings. Slightly shyly, he had at once asked the girl there, who was a little older than he was, to take him to the top of the building so that he could see how high it was, and she answered him with a smile, stretching out her hand. Not knowing what to do with it, he left it dangling in the air, making her mother, who was standing beside them in the kitchen, laugh.

They walked up the stairs, which were strewn with sand, mud, and pieces of wood full of bent rusty nails. He walked cautiously between the obstacles, while she strode confidently in front of him. As her feet hit the pieces of wood, they would turn over, or else stick up in the air then fall on top of one another again, with a noise that made his whole body tremble.

There were three and a half stories jutting up into a sky full of gray clouds the color of concrete. He threw his body onto the roof, thrusting it towards the edge with his eyes on the ground far below. He told her that what he saw was the tiniest, smallest thing he had ever seen, and that this was the highest point he had ever been to in his life, though he was becoming increasingly confused about what those small red spots in the far-off fields might be. As they were coming down the stairs, between the third and second stories, she took his hand and thrust it inside her red underwear. When he tried to withdraw it a few moments later, she pulled it back again, keeping it in the same place, where it was warm. They were happily in love with one another.

Strawberries, strawberries. They hurried down from the third floor and headed for the field with the small red points, which suddenly changed into strawberries. They started to rummage through the soft brown earth, their hands wandering among the green leaves. The strawberries that they picked were still warm from the sun, though it had been hiding for a time behind the clouds—just like his hand, which to this moment preserves the memory of the warmth of her triangle discovered on the third-floor steps.

As the day ended, he kissed her, and they said goodbye to each other. She was standing beside her parents and he beside his father. Their hands lay submissively in the hands of their parents, but there was love hidden in their eyes.

How he loved her. He had also stolen a toy from her, a little elephant carrying a drum, but when he got home he couldn't find it. She had returned and stolen it back from him, how and when he didn't know.

What had happened to that staircase, he wondered, as his eyes fell once again on the remains of the collapsed staircase still impressed on the building on his left.

This woman in front of him, soon she would also disappear from his life, after a few meters. Five meters, he was quite certain. Should he start a conversation with her? Ask her politely what the time was, then ask her if she would allow him to sit beside her on the bench for a little? Yes, he wanted to discuss something important with her, tell her about last night's dream, open his heart to her, then she would open her heart to him. He would tell her what a lonely life he had. But what if she started to abuse him? Most likely, she would regard his behavior as disagreeable, if not actual harassment, and would assemble a collection of people to give evidence against him, so that he would be exposed. He might even lose his job. Goodness! His contribution to the history of mankind would come to an end, together with everything that depended on him, like arranging the different products on the shelves in the store, helping customers find a bag of salt or a sponge for cleaning the pots and pans. Then, who knows, his family might hear of it, and wash their hands of him. His family! At least that way he wouldn't need to hide or lie to them anymore. It would be better if they discovered everything, wouldn't it? And he in turn would give in to the fact that he was a total loser. He suddenly felt extremely tired; tired of the whirlpools of thoughts that he didn't know how to stop, or stop himself thinking them. How he missed being young, when he didn't think of the past at all, but rather of the future. The only things to come into his head now were events from the past that just added to his frustration. When he was young he had dreamed of becoming an archaeologist, and now he could only keep recalling how he had not become one. One didn't even need a "good" grade to study archaeology at university. One simply had to pass. But even this had become difficult to achieve as time went on, and he no longer succeeded at all. Seven years, and he hadn't yet met the requirements of the third year at university. A terrible failure, there could be no doubt about it. But at least his work in the supermarket allowed him to provide for himself, and for the hours that he spent gloomily in his room. He had changed a lot. His silence had become more oppressive, and not just because he was shy, but because he no longer had any desire for conversation. Nothing now came out of his mouth except his breath. When he had started work in the supermarket, he would respond if someone greeted him, with a smile that stayed with him as he listened to a customer's question, then went with him or her, and found an answer on one of the shelves. And when a customer had a problem with some produce that he would have to rearrange later, he would calm him down and reassure him. At other times he would exchange short sentences with some of them about the tiresomeness of the day—not his own, of course—the state of the weather, the cost of living and similar subjects. But now he would not even look at the questioner: he would just point at the area where the answer could be found, and that was that. The supermarket had completely finished him, and his tongue. The cold blast that came from the air conditioner to keep the produce from rotting had completely rotted his soul. Until she had come along, and repeated her greeting insistently: "I said hello."

He raised his head, slightly confused, and his eyes came to rest on a pretty girl. He hurriedly painted a false smile on his face so that she would not imagine she had charmed him, though that was exactly what had happened. When she asked him for some non-foaming shampoo, he went on rearranging the tins of corn beside the tins of peas, and told her that the beauty products section was on the second floor, and that the shampoo shelf was at the front on the right. She spoke to him again, more firmly this time, saying that she would prefer it if he looked at her while he was speaking to her. He raised his head and smiled again, a more convincing smile this time, saying he would be happy to look at her beautiful face. A wave of warmth swept right through his body. He hadn't meant it; he didn't know how those words had escaped from his lips, or where he had heard or read them, maybe in a film script, for that sort of expression was certainly not his own. Even if he and his entire family had worked at it for the rest of their lives, they wouldn't have come up with even the first half of a phrase like that. To salvage the situation, then, he told her that he would take her there himself. He walked in front of her, praying to God that the girl would not complain about him, and promising that this would be the last time he treated anyone like that. Then he added that he wouldn't be like those opportunists who prayed to God, then forgot him after their demands had been fulfilled. No, he wouldn't do that, he would remember him and thank him.

After walking for a few minutes, he heard her say "Thank you" from behind. She wasn't going to complain about him, then. He thanked God from the depths of his heart.

But could anything happen between them? He could sense something. Or was he exaggerating? Could he let his imagination run wild like this, just because she hadn't complained? Shame on him! But nothing was going to stop him from dreaming, so he walked in front of her to the beauty products shelf, just as he had walked to his first love on the third floor.

They started to look for non-foaming shampoo together, like two old friends. Then, as their search went on, she was forced to confess that the reason she wanted it was because she didn't even have the energy to rinse the foam out of her hair.

This incident, quite unconnected with his desires or dreams, was roughly why he came to find himself in her house. He sat there with a stunned look, not moving from his place, like a lizard sleeping in the shade of a roof on a blazing hot day. She took his hand and moved it over her breast, then the rest of her body, drowning him in a soft, warm desire he had never known existed in this world. Then he pounced on her.

How beautiful for his hand to feel a warm, living body answering to the pressure of his fingers. He had lost hope of holding anything except for tin cans and bags of produce. This was a heart, not the hum of a meat freezer. This was hair, not a brush!

He loved her, he loved her hair that was tired of carrying soap foam, he loved the quivering of her body under his fingers. He loved this body that his fingers were clutching at, giving him new life as they moved over it. He remembered his first love and moved down below her belly, caressing her with his fingers so that she gasped. Then he went down further, where he encountered a damp warmth, then still further, till he was going where he had never explored before, and there, he caught his breath at the sound coming from deep inside her, reminding him of the sound of his mother coming in from the balcony with her black plastic sandals that slipped with every movement of her damp feet, preceded by a stream of rinse water with a light soapy foam floating on top of it. Now he was pulling himself forward with his fingers to where he had never been before. Overwhelmed by love, he could no longer go on. He pressed her under his fingers, losing himself in her, praying that no one would find him and separate him from her, but she shouted, and pushed his hand roughly away from her, then laughed at him and said: "Not like that! You're hurting me."

As he moved his hand away, a great wave of cold swept over him, like the cold he was used to from the air conditioning in the store. As he apologized, she laughed again, took his hand and said that he was hurting her, and that he should be gentler. He said sorry again, and gently let go of her hand. For a few moments neither of them said anything, then he put on his clothes and left.

She never returned to the store, and he had only the memory of her, and his hatred of himself and perhaps of her as well. Of her laughter and his clumsiness. But how could he have learned how to hold a woman? Certainly not from his mother, who had never ever shown him, her son, as much love and tenderness as she showed the plastic flowers when she picked them up to clean them.

Her smell has stayed with him until this day under his fingernails, and it sometimes passes under his nose without his knowing where it has come from. And at night, whenever he wakes, even for a brief moment, she is the first thing that comes into his mind. He eagerly awaits the day when he will wake up and not find that she is the first thing to appear before his eyes and the only thing he can remember the whole day long. He will tell her everything, this woman on the bench, he will tell her that he has known two women before. Then he will ask her not to rush to judge him. And to share his dream with him.

Suddenly, like the twinkling of an eye, everything went dark then light again. He raised his eyes to the sky and saw a small cloud hurrying away from the sun. It must be a strong wind, then. He turned his eyes towards her again and this time noticed a touch of blue on her face, possibly also from the cold. But the hair that the wind had almost pulled out of place several meters ago now hung down freely beside her ears. She hadn't turned in his direction even once. There were still two meters between them. He kept on walking, with her in front of him, and the nearer he came to her, the more resigned he felt.

So the couple of meters left would come to an end, and everything would end. And he would leave it all to end without doing anything.

But what could he do? He thought of catching her foot as he approached her, so that she would trip him up and something would happen. Yes, no, he didn't know.

She herself still seemed distracted. Perhaps she had noticed out of the corner of her eye that he had been staring at her for fifteen meters, and had feigned her absentmindedness so that she could pretend not to notice him. But now he was immediately in front of her.

She didn't turn towards him.

He lowered his eyes and for a fraction of a second—just because of the sun, nothing else—saw their two shadows merging on the square.

"What's the time?"

If only he could have asked her. But he simply repeated the phrase to himself, in a voice stifled by the weight of his back that had witnessed her disappearance, that woman in black he had left sitting on the wooden bench behind him.

The Fourth Measure

As if every beginning is an end,
Just as we begin, an ending comes,
Suddenly, its touch unfelt,
Sweeping us naturally and heedlessly away.

She walked with him to the parking lot, and said goodbye with the words: "It's over."

He started the car engine, whose roar stayed with him the whole way, like a background to that short, simple sentence that began again and repeated itself every time it finished: "It's over!"

Who ended it?

Was it him, her, his mother, her father, his brother, her nephew, her ambitions, his comments, her fumblings, his age, the dryness under her left eye, his baldness, or none of these? Perhaps it had just ended by itself.

No, he couldn't believe that she had said to him: "It's over."

But believe it or not, that was it, everything between them was over. Anyway, he had been expecting it for a long time, the whole time, in fact. He had been full of fear since the beginning. He had tried hard not to give in to it completely, this love that had just ended. That is, if it was possible not to give in to it completely.

Actually, he had never even once believed that she might be in love with him. He had known since the first day that she would not stay with him, for she was much better than him.

She had been exactly as he had imagined every day until one day he met her for the first time. She had a delicate nose, like the ones that most Greek statues had lost in the course of various wars through the ages, as depicted in school history books. Her mouth was delicate as well, while her eyes were of an uncertain color: were they brown, black, or amber? Her fine nails led into slender fingers, while the hand they were joined to stretched out over a body that made a half circle when it lay in bed. Her wavy hair filled the pillow, taking it up completely and leaving no space for his head.

Suddenly, no more than thirty-five kilometers since they had parted, he was overcome by a powerful longing for her. He wished she could be here at his side, for him to clasp her to his chest and not let her go forever.

When she ate straight from the pot, and he told her that it wasn't right, why had he said anything? When he was reading one evening and she told him she wanted him, he told her to wait until the end of the paragraph, but he never finished it because he no longer wanted anything in the world except her, and her desire for him. But although he reached the supposed end of the paragraph, she no longer wanted him, and when he made that comment about the pot, she no longer wanted to eat, and when he started to tell her how in love he was, she no longer replied. He couldn't even make her laugh anymore.

But what was the use of all this if love had ended? It was over, then.

Perhaps the end had started when she complained to him one morning, saying: "You love me too much."

She knew because she loved him less.

After that she started enumerating all his faults, though he already knew them well enough himself. First, his age: he could easily have been her father. Second, he asked so many questions that it got on her nerves. Third, there was a lot of hair on his body. And sex: it had never been very good, and then he couldn't manage it at all. Fourth, he had a weak personality; he was easily influenced by others, which showed a lack of character. And fifth, frankly, he was no good at anything.

His one remaining virtue, so it appeared, was that he was breathing.

He knocked on a friend's door, and when she asked him how he was, he replied: "Bad."

This was the first thing he had said after hearing the words "It's over."

She turned the word "Bad" over in her mouth several times without adding a single other word to it. He told her what had happened. He was hoping she would embrace him and say: "It's alright, my friend, I'll go to her and persuade her to come back to you." But she didn't say that, didn't make any suggestions, and didn't seem to be bothered at all, as if not caring was the most natural thing to do in the face of his misfortune.

Was he so bad that his grief should be met with no reaction? Could she not stand him anymore either? He asked her, and she confirmed it. He was no longer bearable, and she could well understand how his girlfriend's love for him had ended.

He slammed the door behind him. As he was going down the stairs on the way out of the house he wished that the staircase would never end, and that he would never arrive anywhere.

But had she really left him? Perhaps it was because there was still some hope inside him, protecting him from the most terrible pain, that he was not completely shattered.

He couldn't imagine her not being there among all the people he would see, or that he wouldn't hear her voice among all those reaching his ears. Impossible, he had to do something, talk to her, persuade her. It was unbelievable that everything should end this easily.

But he soon heard her again quite clearly, whispering behind his back "It's over," and he nearly went mad.

Abduct her, then, and press a revolver into her back, so that she would love him again.

Her back had been like an apricot at the height of summer, covered with a fine layer of pale, slender hairs, with small brown freckles scattered among them, as if they were taking a stroll. Sometimes he no longer wanted to touch her, for his body was too rough.

He would kill her, but before he killed her he would thank her for their love. He would have to kill her, because she wouldn't agree to come back to him when he brought his revolver close to the apricot.

Then what?

He wouldn't be breathing the air she had breathed. He wouldn't be leaning on the wall she had glanced at for a moment as she walked away from him.

He put the revolver out of his mind, and wished he were dead. It would have been better to have let himself be strangled in her hair the last night she had left it spread on the pillow, before walking beside him on that dry night with its velvety air and telling him as they reached the car: "It's over."

So he went on, every day, every minute, trying to resist his desire to be with her, though he often failed. He would find his fingers pouncing on the telephone, on the keys that made up her seven-digit number. He would press them so fast that they would make a pitiful tune, pouring into his despairing ear to be followed by a slow ringing. And between every ring and the next, the pain in his heart grew worse.

As soon as she realized that it was him calling, she would put the receiver down in his face without a moment's hesitation. After that, she would no longer even answer. Why should she answer, when it was all over?

But his love for her was not over, and never would be. Not at all, it was all he had. Whether she liked it or not, he would keep loving her. He loved her, nothing more.

The Fifth Measure

As if every beginning is an end,
Just as we begin, an ending comes,
Suddenly, its touch unfelt,
Sweeping us naturally and heedlessly away.
Yet for us, it's not easy to end

I promise you and I promise myself that I won't dis-
turb you anymore. I've never tried that, but I'm suf-
fering a lot because you're not replying to me. Still, it's
not important; it's not your problem. All I want to
know is why. Why the hatred?

Please try to explain, and if you can't, thank you,
and good luck.

I promise you again that these are the last words
you will hear from me, ever.

Should she believe him?

But how could she believe him? The idea that
she had to believe him shattered her. Just reading
his words was enough to destroy her and fill her

with fear. *I promise you and I promise myself...* Lies. Cheap, fake words.

Pain spread through her teeth. It was enough for her to realize how much she hated him, so that nothing was bearable any longer.

She hoped he would not disturb her again. But so long as he could succeed in reaching her, in fact, so long as he was alive, so long as he was capable of hurting her... The knowledge that he was driving his car away in the darkness at this very moment made her heart sink. She would dream of him tonight. She would see him looking strong, with submissive eyes to spite her, while her own body would be consumed by weakness. Faced with her total impotence before the darkness of the night into which he had just disappeared, and the memory of all those days they had spent together, she almost burst into tears. She really shouldn't have done it. She couldn't believe that he had one day held her body. Her head hurt when she recalled how he had once clutched at her hair when they slept together. Had she once fallen in love with him, only for him to now come and ask: "Why the hatred?" She couldn't for a moment recall a single moment of the love he was presuming. But she hated herself for feigning love towards him—a love he had believed in. She hadn't loved him. It was impossible for her to have loved him. He had just been beside her as anyone else might have been, and they had spent time together, because she'd had the time anyway. They may have somehow been close, for they had lived together for some time, and he sometimes took her out. But she was always looking in the opposite direction. Looking out of the window towards the road, or smoking. She remembers it well; she didn't turn towards him, so that the smoke wouldn't go in his direction. She liked to look and blow the smoke away. He was nothing to her, and she didn't ask to be anything to him. When she had proposed marriage, it was because she wanted to improve his life: she wanted to renovate his house, repaint it, and replace the broken doors. But for him to believe that she loved him was a mistake. She just loved order, and didn't like chaos. Chaos might be trendy and refined, but she herself couldn't stand it. An orderly and well-regulated life might be sad, but at the end of the day, never mind. Basically, with him, with someone else, or without anyone, it was all the same, but living with someone would be somehow amusing. Loneliness was hard, she had never gotten used to it, and never would. With no one around her she felt that her life was passing in vain and her time was slowly disappearing. And because she couldn't stand being alone, there had been a relationship between them. She hadn't loved him. How could anyone believe that she had? It had just been something to bring some life into her life. He would ring the bell, and then start to turn the key in the door. Sometimes she would like to lie silently in bed while it was dark outside, then suddenly hear the sound of the key turning in the lock. That had been nice. But later she couldn't stand him any longer. When she insisted they split up, she had already reached the stage when she didn't just want him to leave her, she wanted him to leave her alone. He, as a project, no longer interested her. She had lost all hope in him, so she said: "It's over," and when something is over, it's over. That's life; no one can be forced by anyone else. But the problem was that he had been a horrible person from the start, although she hadn't noticed any of it at the time, since she hadn't dealt with him with enough concentration or depth. Anyway, why should she have?

Perhaps it would have been better if he had left her. But she had waited and waited and he didn't do anything, so she left him. This was quite natural, especially after the relationship had petered out. He himself hadn't wanted to split up, or perhaps he hadn't fully comprehended the situation, and this rather surprised her. In any case, it seems that he had become attached to her, and so she had continued to be kind to him, despite being bored and fed up with him and his insistent attitude. For a long time she had begged him to leave her, on the basis that they weren't compatible; because she was confused at the moment; because she was frustrated; because he was better than her. Perhaps for all of those reasons, she wasn't capable of confronting him, perhaps also because the pair of them might one day have some common interest, who knows? As time went on, she had come to the conclusion that the best way to deal with his never-ending telephone calls was by ignoring them completely, as if it were a wrong number or something of the sort. She succeeded in preserving her nervous composure for several months until that night during September when he'd called her at two in the morning. She could be slow in her reactions at any time and for any reason, except for someone waking her, and particularly a telephone ringing. From the other end of the line, he told her that he wanted to see her. She replied that it was two in the morning, and why should he call her at a time like this? When he told her he loved her, she replied that she didn't give a shit for him and his love, that he was never ever to call her again, and she'd had enough of his crap. Then she hung up the phone. It was two in the morning and her body was shivering. The next minute he called again and told her that she didn't deserve all this love that he felt for her, and that he wanted back all the letters he had sent her, right now. She told him it would be easier to move a mountain from one place to another than to ask her for the letters. She wouldn't give them to him. Then she'd put the receiver down, and pulled the phone line out of the wall. It was sheer good fortune that she didn't break the receiver. She couldn't go back to sleep. She got up from her bed and started rummaging through her papers, gathering together his letters and photos, and separating them from the rest.

In one of the photos of the two of them together, he was resting his hand on her shoulder, they were both laughing, and she was putting her hand over her mouth to hide her teeth. The shirt she was wearing was beautiful then, but was now shabby. In another photo of the pair of them she could be seen in his arms wearing a brown leather coat. She looked very happy in both pictures, but she didn't believe she had been: either she was smiling for the camera, or she was stupid. There were several other pictures of him. She didn't understand what he wanted from her, and hoped he wouldn't contact her again.

Then she started opening letters from other men and sifting through their photos. Most of the letters she had received in the last ten years were intended to make her feel guilty. None of the men who had sent her chiding letters of this sort—or others, for that matter—had sent her even a single bunch of roses. Anyway, she didn't understand these men, and couldn't even decipher the hand-writing in their letters. She didn't know why they had bothered to write them. Quite naturally, she didn't care about them. Or rather, she had to exert a lot of effort in order to care about them, or those that had written them in the first place. Sometimes, when she looked around her, she couldn't believe, or know, how people could care about each other so spontaneously. Her mother, her father, her brother, her friends, with all their concern for their families and sometimes for her. It was as if she didn't know how to love, and when she tried, she did it clumsily. But as time went on she had no longer tried to battle this trait of hers, and had started to be satisfied with what she could get from short encounters with different people.

She liked someone to drive her in his car, take her into his bed, and give her his clothes. When these people went out, leaving her alone in their homes, she liked to wander around among their things. She enjoyed this lack of familiarity with her surroundings, and savored the experience of this sort of personal museum. She would tidy the house a bit, wash the dishes and maybe empty the fridge of rotten vegetables. They would call around eleven o'clock and ask her whether everything was alright. Then she'd get dressed and leave. She preferred to leave. She might be embarrassed to meet them again; she wouldn't know how to behave. She would be confused. She liked her encounters to be like furtive spring matings. But with him she had made a mistake. She had made an even bigger mistake when she had given him a copy of her house key. She didn't know what had come into her mind to make her suddenly do that. Perhaps she had just taken pity on the aged key cutter and wanted to increase his meager salary. But she paid a heavy price, especially when she began to feel bored with him and allow herself to go out with other men. The copy of the key in his possession made her increasingly fearful. This fear started to disgust her later, when one night one of her lovers had to flee the house, when some car lights were reflected on the sitting room wall, and they thought that it must be him. Under pressure, the idiot took one of her socks by mistake, leaving the other sock to remind her of her feeling of suffocation—a feeling that was only to increase as time went on, especially when he started bringing things into the house as if it was his own. When she asked him "What's this?" he wouldn't respond, but would simply open the bag in front of her to show her what was in it, with a smile of self-satisfaction, then start to laugh loudly. How dreadful! Until one day, finally, eureka! She had telephoned him and proposed marriage, but he refused. She then told him that she couldn't go on any longer with their relationship because of social pressure. At the time, although she hadn't really wanted to marry him and her proposal had been just a strategy for splitting up, his refusal hurt her a little. She remembered how she had sat down on the chair that day under the light in the corridor separating the rooms, as the silence grew more intense. She'd felt completely sad, because not only did she not love anyone, but no one loved her either. No one at all. This lack of love was no longer a game resulting from her warped sense of humor, but a living reality embodied in the one person she had ever given a copy of her house key.

Then she stood up and told herself it didn't matter. The story was over as far as she was concerned, and she didn't need to worry about him anymore, especially after he'd refused to marry her. So she was finally able to tell him, clearly and politely, "It's over." But instead, he had started calling her and leaving her messages on her answering machine every day. She didn't reply, and didn't know whether he'd noticed that she didn't reply. Then it all became tiresome for her, but she didn't want to hurt him by telling him to get lost. After that, he started coming to the café where she usually sat, and left messages for her on the notepad the waiter used to jot down the customers' orders, until she got extremely fed up. She continued to avoid him as much as possible, hoping that he would leave her alone soon, and she no longer answered the phone. She still didn't understand what he wanted from her. But that night, after he had caught her automatically answering the phone in her sleep without thinking, she felt that all her kindness and indifference had been exhausted, and her fatigue turned into disgust and fear.

Some weeks after he had called that night, he called her at five in the morning and started berating her. She cut him off, her heart racing.

Outside, the darkness was still stronger than the morning light. She pulled the phone wire from the wall and started to cry. From that night on and forever, she would always disconnect the telephone before settling down to sleep, and if she left it connected, she would feel as if she were completely naked. But even disconnecting the phone didn't prevent the formation of a profound sorrow, anxiety, cynicism and contempt both towards him and towards herself.

Some days later she went home and found a voice message that he had left for her, reproaching her for forgetting all the times they'd spent together. She had gone crazy, and started hitting the telephone against the ground like a madwoman, as if his voice was inhabiting the phone, until she realized that if she went on like that she would have to buy a new handset. So she left it on the ground, and started to cry, this time because a thought like the last one could possibly go through her head during such a difficult time. How worthless she was. She cried until she groaned like an animal aware of a great evil surrounding it, aware also that the source of evil was itself. Afterwards she washed the tears from her face, without drying the water on her eyes, where some drops remained, preventing her from seeing the world clearly. Then she went out into the garden, where the sun might console her a little.

Under the rays of the sun she realized how she had been running to hide from him for a long time. She had no longer answered the telephone, or gone anywhere where there was the faintest possibility that he might visit as well. Like presidential security, she would check any place she was about to enter, to be certain he was not there. This was what she had come to: absolute terror. She went back inside and picked up the phone, but it was broken. She shut the front door behind her and started to look for a public telephone. She found one, and ignoring the strong smell of urine around it, called him. She had to call him. She got through and the telephone rang, but no one replied. Then the answering machine responded, with his hateful voice. After the beep she said: "Wipe my phone number from your memory." Then she went back home and waited for time to pass. Pass and pass until there was another life. The telephone beside her was dead, and its death comforted her.

Little by little the darkness began to lift, though sleep was still far out of reach. Then the morning light crept in through the white curtains, making the contents of the house appear less sharp than usual. Meanwhile, the sound of the dawn call to prayer began to spread through the house. Wherever she went, there would always be the beautiful sound of the call to prayer.

The days had passed calmly again, until one day she had come home, put her bag down near the sofa, and gone into the bathroom. When she returned to the sitting room she pressed the button on the answering machine and found one message. She listened to it again. His voice was calm, deep, clear, and perhaps smiling. She listened a third time. He was saying that he was going to rape her, then added in a deeper voice that this was the only thing that would satisfy his lust. He was smiling in his lust. She sat down on the sofa and looked at the telephone with its twisted cord, following it with her eyes from beginning to end once, then again. Then she reached out toward the spirals of wire, and tried to wrap them all around her fingers, but they slipped off the surface of her nails, so she tried repeatedly to get them back over all her fingers. When she had succeeded, she went on opening and closing her hand, the pressure of the wire circles tightening around her fingers, occasionally pulling out some of the little hairs on them. He was smiling. After a short while, darkness covered her eyes. She wanted to go out to see the night: she wanted to go out, but her whole body had suc-cumbed to weakness. Only her fingers inside the spiral telephone cord were able to move.

There was always something to suggest the beginning of hatred inside her. From the very first moment she would notice the ray of hatred, or perhaps it was this that drew her to those around her. At first she would believe that it was not real, a hasty judgment or an imagined feeling, so she would try to ignore it, but it would return a second and third time until it would take possession of her, and she would no longer be capable of bear-ing it. So she would wait for them to leave her; she would wait and wait until she herself ran away, one way or another. At the end of the tunnel there would always be another story, a new love, to revive her. But someone had come who did not accept the ending. And so the darkness of the tunnel had extended until it had now taken over everything she could see.

So her body was to be his means of revenge. She looked at it, this thing that he was using to threaten her. Her body, her constant companion, by whose means she lived. She stood up and went out into the garden, where she found a warm night and thick darkness, especially beside the olive trees. She looked at her hands, and despite the darkness of the night, she noticed the marks from the telephone cord on her fingers. Her hands were shaking. Where was she to go?

She'd woken the following morning with a great feeling of fear inside her, which then accompanied every idea that crossed her mind. She was not just afraid of him, but of everything. All her attempts to outmaneuver her feeling of fear and threat had disintegrated. Nothing could penetrate this feeling. He would rape her. No one could help her. The police would not do anything, nor her friends, nor her family; no one. She had always known that she was alone but it was only now that she realized how alone she really was. She would never be able to defend herself against him. She took off her underwear and started to look at the thing that had become a site of threat and torment, but she couldn't go on looking. She hated it. All she wanted now was to burn it, to light a fire in her body. Then she started to cry. For several days she did not wash. Her nights were full of fitful sleep, and of dreams that she could no longer distinguish from reality. In her dreams he passed in front of her, pursuing her as she fled. He would touch her and she would be unable to push his hands off her, unable to defend herself or even to scream. Fear would paralyze her, while he did whatever he liked with her body, calmly and naturally. The days and nights turned into a single lump of pain that she could no longer bear. Every day that passed was weighed down by the anticipation that he would show up and carry out his threat.

And one night, while she was lying in her bed, she felt that he was looking at her from the window. She could even see his face through the glass, although it was all mixed up with the reflection of clothes hung opposite the window. His face looked pale blue. Then she heard footsteps. She stopped breathing, or perhaps her breath stopped of its own accord. She tried to remember whether she had locked the front door. Had she locked it? Could he break it down? She was overcome by a sense of numbness that enveloped every part of her body. He was watching her. He could see her in the lighted room behind the glass. She moved her hand, stretching it slowly towards the light beside her, turned it off, then moved her hand back beside her. She stayed sitting in the same position with nothing but silence ringing in her ears.

Gradually, as dawn approached and it became possible to see outside again from the room, her terror began to subside. From the window she could see birds hopping between the branches of the dried-up almond tree. She couldn't comprehend the night she had just spent nor the morning that was coming, and how many nights and mornings like these would she spend in her life. She went out to the garden. Before she went out, she had picked up a knife, but she left it on the table in the sitting room.

Outside, dew covered the garden table. The slow appearance of the morning light restored her regular breathing. But she didn't want to breathe, she wanted to die.

She went back to bed and found the sheets cold. The cold sent a shiver through her whole body. Enveloped in this feeling, she warmed herself with the idea of setting him alight. She would burn his face and his hands, his tongue, and finally his penis. The following evening, she didn't turn on the lights in any of the rooms in the house. She sat in the sitting room looking at the pale reflection of the lights from the cars in the distance on the wall beside her. In the past she had sat on the same couch waiting for the headlights of his car. Now the mere possibility of his being nearby in the darkness shattered her. If only it would end quickly, this darkness, but there was nothing to end it, just a long, lonely night. Beside her, for three full hours, the ringing of the telephone came and went. She would lift the receiver, but only silence would come from the other end; his silence. If only he would come, and the waiting end. She would turn her eyes away from the scene while he was raping her. She would let him rape her. A small victim of his torment, and of her contempt for him and the rest of the world. The important thing was not to see him. She would close her eyes, and he would reach his climax, then leave her forever. She had no other choice.

Or perhaps she would run away, and start a new life somewhere else. Perhaps that was the only solution. She had to move out of this house, at least move away from its memories, and the terror that had now started to inhabit its walls.

In the space of two weeks she had moved to a new house, a new town, and a new telephone number, which she had ordered from a company that was also new. But although she started to enjoy some quiet during her days, her nights were not ready to give up their terror. They were full of dreams about him. She would see him in an open shirt, through which she could glimpse his soft, dark skin and his bony chest. She wanted to stick a knife in there hard, but she wouldn't do it. He would come closer and closer and almost grab her, while she did nothing. Total paralysis.

Some days later, while she was sitting on the balcony of her new house, busy with some papers and boxes, the telephone rang. She picked up the receiver, but there was silence. She went back to the balcony. She sat on a box, and her heartbeats began to choke her, their very rhythm suffocating her. Then she noticed a walnut tree planted at the far end of the garden. Most of its branches hung over the street behind the wall of her house. The tree was beautiful, while her own life was hateful and filthy, and it would always be like that. She looked at the boxes; at least she hadn't emptied them yet. She stayed sitting there as the sun began to move away slowly to the west. Then the sunset breeze started to blow over the walnut tree, moving its dry leaves in soft, sensual movements, and she froze. She could no longer say this kind of thing, or even think about it, or her sexual desires. She could no longer go near that terrifying area. No one had come near her body for a long time. As the shadows grew longer, the leaves on the walnut tree moved faster, and some of them escaped the branches and flew far, far away beyond the wall, until everything disappeared into the night.

She would kill him. So long as he was alive, she would not to able to live. His mere existence in the land of the living was bringing her infinite pain, and she had to put an end to it. Finally, as she paced up and down in the house, the night began to seem less oppressive. If he came to her she would kill him with the knife. The knife was lying on the table in front of her. She would conceal it in her hand, and just as he was about to rape her, when he was very close to her, she would push it into the middle of his neck from behind, and hold it there until he was dead. By law, she would be defending herself, while he would no longer be alive. She would live a life completely free of him. She wouldn't accept the weakness of her body any longer. She would kill him. Or perhaps a car accident, which she could help with. The brakes. Or burn him alive in the car. Or she could put a bomb in his bed. First of all, she had to find out where he was living. She would wait for him in the darkness, go up to him, shoot him and it would be all over. He would collapse, then she would shoot him again, to be sure. But where would she get a revolver? She would have to wear black, and carry a gag. She would buy one. She would follow him for a while. Would she have to see him, then? All her imaginary strength dispersed as she visualized him in front of her; her weakness and fear came back to her again, and she began to cry. Why wouldn't he just stop, without her killing him? Forget her. Die of his own accord. God, if only he'd die. Every time she thought he'd forgotten her, he would appear again, so she would convince herself that it was the last time. She was full of sick hopes. There was always a new hope that everything would be alright. But nothing was alright, and it never had been.

Suddenly she heard a light tap at the door. She asked who it was. No one replied. But she felt there was definitely someone there behind the door. Him. She could feel him. He knocked at the door again, but this time she didn't ask who it was. He had managed to find her. Should she open the door to him, so that he would rape her and she would kill him? She moved away from the door, toward the table where the knife was. For a few moments she stood in front of it, then went back to the door. He was still there. The tension increased. She was in front of him. They were both here, less than half a meter apart, with only the door separating them.

She stayed where she was for some time, unable to move. Then she put her hand out to the door and opened it. There was no one there. There was only the darkness and that short note.

The Sixth Measure

As if every beginning is an end,
Just as we begin, an ending comes,
Suddenly, its touch unfelt,
Sweeping us naturally and heedlessly away.
Yet for us, it's not easy to end
Except when there's no place left for love.

"Sweetheart."

"My sweetheart."

"My sweetheart."

"My sweetheart."

"When can I see you?"

"I miss you."

"When can we meet?"

"Just come."

"Do you miss me?"

Then, "Are your breasts getting bigger?"

And then, "How's the baby?"

"The bastard. What kind of man doesn't love his own son? Even a dog feels something for its young. He's worse than a dog."

"The bastard broke the phone? That's the third time. I'll get you a new one."

"No, I don't have one."

"I'm telling you I don't have one. It was stolen and the bank couldn't do anything, so I canceled it."

"No, I don't have one, don't you understand?"

"That's enough, Shahinaz, no, no, I'm telling you, no! I don't have one."

"Alright, I've got to go now. I'll see you tomorrow. Leave your car downtown, and we'll go from there together. Alright? Alright?"

That was my father whispering into the phone outside my closed bedroom door.

I listened to him whispering with a tenderness I'd never heard before. Meanwhile, I was trying to keep my breaths as short as possible, as my chest hurt each time I took in air. He sounded tender and sweet. Where had he gotten this voice from, and when did he learn it, if he'd never used it before in his life?

I could hear my father talking about breasts as if he were discussing shares rising on the stock market.

He doesn't even know the way to the sea. Yet he seems to know that a woman's breasts get bigger when she's pregnant.

Trapped behind the closed door by my illness, and forced to listen to his conversation, I was as powerless to control my rising temperature as I was to resist the arousing sensation his explicit words had on my body. I followed this sensation as it spread through me carelessly, until his question about the baby brought me back to my senses. I was frightened. But I instantly realized that my fear of a potential brother related to purely practical concerns: the possibility of having to split our future inheritance with a fourth person, who might even take the largest share of my father's money. After all, his mother had been able to bring out a tenderness in my father that my mother, brother, sister, and I had failed to extract from him over all these years. However, this fear vanished, leaving only pain, the moment I heard him mention another man. I realized that it was not my dad who was the baby's father; it was this other man, the one who had broken the phone three times and was even worse than a dog.

The conversation about the bank card returned me to a sickly calm. For all his explicit, loving words, he was still as stingy as ever. Then, when he started to lose patience towards the end of the call, he was my father again. He never had the energy to listen to any of us. And now she had become one of us.

He hung up and left. A familiar cold silence returned to fill the house once more.

But he had seen enough Egyptian soap operas to know well that she was not his sweetheart and he was not her sweetheart, so how could he have fallen into this trap?

But I too had seen enough soap operas, so what if the baby were my brother and even looked like me? What would I do with a brother like that? In reality, I'd always felt a close affinity with all the wretched of the earth, be they thieves, whores, or tramps. But now that it was no longer an affinity based on mere theory but on reality, in which I was connected with a brother who shared a father with me, I felt utter revulsion for the wretched Shahinaz. So I wouldn't go with her to the hospital for the delivery, and I wouldn't stand in the corridor listening to her scream as she gave birth to my half-brother. I didn't even know, if I had the choice, whether I would choose that this child should be born or not. I didn't know either if I would like to take this potential brother to the zoo, or out into the country. He'd pick a flower, push it in his mouth, then spit it back out, staring up at me with tearful eyes that betrayed its horrible taste—eyes that might resemble my own, inherited from my father. No.

I slept, then woke to a feeling of cold. My hair and my forehead were wet with sweat, and my eyes and face were wet with tears.

My father.

The first drop of tears fell onto the pillow reluctantly, but those that followed fell with extraordinary ease, settling together in one damp spot, which began by my cheeks and spread out to the sides. At first, the damp pillow was a little warm, but after a few moments it turned cold, painfully cold, so I turned my head in the other direction to avoid it. The tears now changed course and started to trickle from the corners of the eyes across the nose, before slopingdiagonally along the cheek, falling into the ear and a moment later onto the pillow. I was tired. I felt heavy and irritated by my tears, though they had now begun to slow.

Outside, it was raining. I followed the raindrops' flow on the window screen. Like the tears, each new drop landed in the same spot and followed the path carved for it by the preceding one. Each drop was separated from the next by only a few small squares as it made its way through the mesh, until it reached the bottom of the window. How did each drop manage to land on the screen in the very same spot that the first drop had chosen? The interval between the raindrops was the same as that between my tears. I wasn't imagining this. I hadn't imagined the conversation on the other side of the door.

I was convulsed by tears, they burned my face, making me want to tear at it. I didn't want to lose my mind, I wasn't mad, how could I hold on to my senses?

I slept again.

There was the coldness of the sweat beneath me, and the coldness of the tears on the pillow. I remember that I cried. I remember the conversation.

The sound of the Syrian soap on the television could just be heard through the patter of the raindrops. If the television hadn't been on, the patter of the rain would have been the only sound audible as background to my sadness.

Suddenly, the door of the room opened. It was my father.

He opened the wardrobe, which was no longer my own wardrobe since I had left home. He and my mother had put things in it that had nothing to do with each other or with anyone at all.

I looked back up at the ceiling. I knew from the noise that what he had taken out of the wardrobe must be sweets, most likely peppermints. No one likes peppermints; that's why he would put them within reach of everyone's hands, knowing no one would ever reach for them. He asked me if I'd like one but I didn't reply.

He stopped for a moment and asked how long I would be staying in bed without consulting a doctor. Again, I didn't reply, and he didn't wait for my reply, and didn't shut the door behind him either.

From time to time a shudder went through my back. It started from the bottom, then spread in circles until it covered it all. I wanted to die, and felt cold and hungry. I hadn't eaten anything since the previous day.

91

If it hadn't been for what had happened, I would have taken a peppermint from him, instead of the taste of sickness that filled my mouth.

He was now leaning on the wall by the door frame, looking at the television, his head in front of me and his arms around his head, while I was thinking what a filthy man he was.

In the morning, he had been an incredible man.

Until that morning, I would sometimes find myself crying because it had occurred to me that he might die. A terrible weakness would overcome me, anticipating the sadness that I knew would inevitably crush me as soon as he died. Several times I had thought of killing myself to escape from this likely tragedy, and I actually tried to do so at least twice. This same pillow that was underneath me now, damp from my tears after the morning's conversation, had been soaked in the past with tears of another kind: tears at the thought of his possible death. How terrified I was at the thought of living without him, without the knowledge that he was still alive somewhere or other. And now I suddenly could, or perhaps it no longer bothered me.

Where had these feelings come from all of a sudden? From one telephone conversation that had lasted two minutes at most, of the total time in the universe. It probably hadn't even reached the minimum length for a call, which would cost less than the smallest peppermint in the cheapest shop. Still, it had made that deep, great, powerful, conquering—and all the rest of the traits of the Almighty—love disappear.

This was the first time I had noticed that he was so old. His hair was thinning, and was almost entirely white, and he had wrinkles all over his neck and hands.

I woke up and found the door of the room closed. I didn't know who had closed it. I stretched out my hand to my genitals and started to masturbate quietly. Then I moved my hand back to my nose, and the smell stirred tears in my eyes.

Go on, cry.

I was woken by a shiver that spread through the lower part of my body, and went down to my knees. It must be a new day. I pulled my body up with difficulty and leaned back against the pillow. When I adjusted it, it showed traces of dried-up tears.

Whenever I moved my head I could feel my brain moving inside it like a bubble of air, like the girl shut up with the dolphin and sparkling drops in the small, transparent plastic container, which I do not know why my brother has kept till this day. I'd try not to move my head. My eyes also hurt when I looked, so I fixed them on the blank wall, then lost all contact with reality.

Once upon a time people died of the common cold, but in the age of science and modern medicine that has become quite rare. But in my case, science and modern medicine had not even set foot in my room, so what was there to prevent my death? Or had they also put an end to the idea of dying from a cold, regardless of the cure? I was talking nonsense. Maybe I was hungry, but I had no appetite.

She'd be sitting at home, and I'd go in. I'd knock on the door, and she'd open it to me. We'd be sitting on the sofa. I'd look at her and she'd look at me. Her children would come, her breasts would swell, and I would have no place among them, while she had taken all the space in my life. I would kill her. Without killing my father. So that he would be as miserable as he'd made me.

I'd knock on the door, I'd sit down, and would find nothing to talk to her about. She probably wouldn't see the resemblance between my eyes and my father's. So I'd leave, and her children would chase me, demanding an explanation, and I'd cry while going down the stairs of her house. Those tears that never stop.

I couldn't stop his words in my head. I couldn't bear my own existence. Words hurt me.

I pulled my feet out from underneath the cover, then my whole body, and felt a dreadful nausea. I opened the door of my room, and found my mother and father sitting silently in the sitting room. I continued on my way towards the kitchen, had a drink, then started to eat everything fit to eat. But the smell of spices as I opened one of the drawers made me want to vomit, and saliva started to build up in my mouth. I tried to hold everything down all the way to the bathroom, then dropped my head over the toilet seat and emptied out everything I had eaten a few moments earlier, as if I were just a vehicle carrying food from the kitchen to the bathroom.

I went back to the kitchen, drank some water, then ate again.

The telephone rang, and I heard my father saying he would be in Jerusalem the following day to attend some meeting.

So he'd be meeting her in Jerusalem. I found some strawberries but they made the saliva well up in my mouth again.

I went back to the sitting room and stood beside my father. This would be the first conversation we had had.

After two days of silence my voice came out tired. "I want to come with you to Jerusalem tomorrow."

"I'm going on business."

"It doesn't matter. I'll wait for you in the car."

"You're not sick any longer?"

"It doesn't matter. I'll wait for you in the car."

"Stop talking such nonsense."

"It doesn't matter. I'm coming."

"You're not coming."

"I am coming, you'll see."

"You're mad."

"I love Jerusalem. I'm coming."

"Stop it right now."

"I'm coming with you, and that's that."

"I won't go to Jerusalem, then."

"I'm coming."

I went into my room and lay down on my bed. What now, would he be wanting me to get even more ill so that I couldn't go with him and ruin his date with Shahinaz?

As we spoke, though, the truth was that the more I insisted on going with him, the less enthusiasm I had for the idea. From now until tomorrow he would have to endure my intimidation. He must be afraid, which amused me, just as it amused me to torment him. At last!

Go to Jerusalem yourself, you and your Shahinaz! And what sort of a name is that, Shahinaz!

I woke with saliva welling up in my mouth. I summoned up as much strength as I could, and leaped out of bed, passing through the sitting room to the balcony, where I sprayed yellow vomit over all the green plants that my mother tended with such love and care. She even dusted them.

I lifted my head to the horizon but I couldn't see my father's car. He must have left early.

As I was smiling at the empty horizon, I felt something, perhaps vomit, running down my nose onto my lip.

I kept standing there, gazing at the vomit running down over the branches of the plants. Should I clean them or should I wait for a rain shower? Better to wash them, rather than rely on the clouds? I didn't have the strength to think any longer, so I left the balcony and went in.

I crossed the sitting room, its pristine air empty of any furniture, and made for my own room, where exhaustion returned to me as soon as I had comprehended the chaos that had taken it over.

I got into bed, hoping that the taste of vomit would disappear from my mouth. A few moments later, I heard my mother call me a bitch from behind the door, because I had buriedmyself in my room ever since coming and hadn't even left it to help her clean the house. Not only that; I'd walked over the floor she'd just cleaned, leaving dirt behind me.

That's all that ever concerned her about my being, nothing else. She had always been like that, my mother. Any mark that I left behind would drive her to the verge of wishing she'd never given birth to me—as indeed, she had certainly wished for some time. Toe prints that barely left any hint of a connection with a foot, and she'd say that I'd made the sitting room dirty.

So she hadn't seen the vomit yet. Or perhaps she'd seen it and not realized what it was, for she'd been totally denying to herself that I'd been sick for two days. That would have required her to offer me love and warmth that she did not have the strength for. It wouldn't be easy for her to give them naturally and instinctively.

She slammed the front door behind her, or perhaps it was just the wind. Then the squeaking of her wet feet in her plastic sandals filled my ears. The sound reminded me of the sound made during intercourse, which made me take the idea of masturbating off the day's agenda. She now began hitting the door with the mop to make me clearly understand that she was cleaning up after me. God bless you, mother. Wow, I couldn't just jump out of bed and kiss her.

The front door of the house banged again, letting in the cold air. Her hands must have been extremely cold, but despite that she carried on with this disgusting cleaning. She just couldn't comprehend that cleaning depressed me far more than dirt, and made me want to be away from her forever. Not to touch her. Then the feeling of nausea and exhaustion overcame me again, so I could no longer breathe. I turned over on my side and vomited onto the carpet beside the bed.

I had now lost my relationship with my mother, forever.

I woke up to find vomit beside me, and could not stop myself from crying.

My mother hadn't entered the room for two days, and she had no reason to enter it now. She wouldn't enter. But she had made terror enter my heart. Even after I had been away from her for such a long time, and become so different from her, despite everything, she was still capable of making terror enter my heart, together with a fear that she would see the vomit on her carpet. Finding out about the vomit would certainly make a greater impact on her than finding out what was going on between my father and that whore. I dragged myself out of bed, wondering where they each would be now. The sitting room was empty. My father hadn't come back yet, and my mother had no doubt run away to avoid the idea of my being ill, which would give me some time to clean the carpet. My father would no doubt come too soon, and she would feel no pleasure at all. But what did all this matter now?

I tried my best, but there were still some traces left. Hair, dust and vomit were all sticking to the dust cloth. So as not to vomit again, I covered my nose and mouth with the end of my sleeve and tried to look at it all dispassionately. How much dispassion it required to be with my family.

I washed the dust cloth, put it back in its place, then washed my hands thoroughly. But I felt everything I'd just cleaned had turned into a smell that was now clinging to me, and my temperature started to go up again. Suddenly, the front door opened again, and a cold breeze came in, followed by my mother. The coolness of the breeze was nice, and seemed able, even in that brief moment, to snatch some of the beads of sweat from my face. My mother, again, muttered that I was a bitch because I'd woken up just now after she'd finished cleaning the house. Then she started on a long speech, the essence of which was that her family, us, that is, and especially me, was filthy, while the rest of the world, and especially its daughters, gave their families love and obedience, relieving them of all their cares and burdens.

I slammed the door in her face, hoping that this might provide a cue to end her speech, but she simply started a new paragraph, albeit a short one, in which she expressed her hope that I would die in a car crash.

I didn't want to die in a car crash. That would be the cruelest way to die. To get into a car and head for your post office box, for example, hoping it would have a nice letter for you, but never arrive because of a car crash that you hadn't planned, and hadn't been planned by the person who killed you, just total insensitivity on the part of the cars concerned.

Then the temperature started to turn into sweat, which would turn cold, then into a bad smell. How many smells were now mingling on my corpse. Vomit, sweat, the smell of masturbation, underarm odors, my feet, the dust rag, my mouth, my hair, my throat, and my tears. Sleep was the only escape from them all.

I wished I were still a child. My mother would have stayed beside me as usual, pushing her horrid lentil soup into my mouth, trying to persuade me each time that this spoonful would taste better than the one before. She would also keep a bowl beside me for me to be sick in.

After I'd vomited, she would force me to take a bath in a tub of cold water, which she would pour over me, while my father stood beside me, encouraging me and spoiling me at the same time.

I woke up to find the door half open. I didn't know who had opened it or come in. Through the glass window, a touch of cold made its way to my neck, provoking a sudden, harsh cough that hurt my chest before slowly subsiding. I hoped I wouldn't have to cough again. I turned my head towards the carpet to check it, and the vomit seemed to have dried. There remained only the smell. I lifted the blanket to sniff my body. Perhaps I liked it a little, this smell.

I coughed again, and again a burning pain spread through my chest, then slowly subsided until it reached its starting point, leaving the field open for a shiver to spread around the base of my spine.

I went out to the kitchen. There was no one in the sitting room, only the television blazing away on its own, with two men on the screen, most likely in their thirties, talking about football.

I looked for some medicine in a small bag beside the coffee machine, and found some strange medicines that made me a little worried about my parents' health. I couldn't find any medicine that could cure me, so I moved to one of the kitchen cabinets where my mother kept sweets.

I took out a biscuit tin, filled a large glass with water, and went back to my room. I shut the door and got into bed, then opened the tin of biscuits and started to devour them. They didn't taste of anything, except for the acidity of the preservatives, which stayed under the tongue and at the top of the throat for a long time. Then I waited for day to turn into night through the window.

After a while, it seemed that the world was refusing to turn dark.

Suddenly there was a knock on a door. Concentrating my thoughts, I could tell that theknocking was on the front door and not the door of my room.

My mother's voice sounded warm and friendly, "Please come in."

The two women sat down. Umm Salim and Salma. Umm Salim was the only woman to visit my mother, as far as I knew, and I didn't think my mother liked her. Their voices were coming from the sitting room while my mother's voice came from the kitchen. They were talking about a little boy that was with them, Salma's son, who was three months old, though my mother said he looked six months. He was huge, and so beautiful! His eyes showed that he had to be one of Umm

Salim's family. The conversation continued around the child without a sound being heard from the child himself, who was so quiet you'd have thought he wasn't really there.

My mother went back to the sitting room accompanied by the clattering of plates. "Please don't put yourself out too much," said the two women, with a brief interval between them, so that it made them seem like a voice and its echo. Then they moved on to a subject that even I could not avoid: Salima's death. Her children were in good health, and the father had married a woman who, fortunately for the orphans, was extremely tenderhearted. I hadn't even expected that Salima would marry, let alone die!

Suddenly, for no apparent reason, Salma laughed, then explained that it was something Salim had said, which I hadn't found funny at all. She must have been trying to change the subject, that's all. But my mother wouldn't let the subject go, recalling how Salima would come to visit my sister and the pair of them would carry on laughing for no reason. As my mother recalled this, Umm Salim expressed her condolences to her and tried to comfort her.

Afaf had used to come with Salima as well, and the three of them would sit on the balcony, whispering together, while I wouldn't be able to make out a single word of what they were saying. Afaf herself had committed suicide during this period. She drank a bottle of cleaning fluid. I often wondered at the time how much it had cost and where it had been before Afaf picked it up and emptied its contents down her throat. Just to calm myself, I imagined it as a blue bottle with a red cover in the cupboard under the sink under the bent waste pipe. And just as the pipe would swallow the waste water, Afaf's throat had swallowed the whole bottle of chloride.

Salima had died two years earlier, following a heart attack that was as unexpected as the news of it, and as the cough that suddenly caught me. Umm Salim asked who it was that had coughed, could it be my father? My mother replied that it was me, and that I'd been sick for three days, during which time I hadn't even left my room. Umm Salim said she hoped I'd be better soon, as did Salma, and they then started talking about the flu, and how suddenly people can get it. They'd had an injection for it this year, like last year, before the beginning of winter. My mother agreed with them, then added that the flu was a terrible thing, especially my flu. I was shocked. I couldn't believe it.

The conversation about the dreadful effects of the flu continued. Everyone had their own recollections of it and of how their temperatures had risen, while Salma compared them with cases she had come across while working in the hospital. My mother asserted that the flu symptoms got worse every year. Meanwhile, my crying got worse every minute. She had no right to talk about me as her sick daughter, she had no right to talk about my illness with such warmth. I'll kill her, I want to kill her. She's killing me.

My mother always had been a hypocrite. She could play the loving mother, but she could never really be one. In front of the world, she was always the heroine of those songs and tunes that would be played on Mother's Day: a woman's life and love; a mother crying with happiness for her child.

She always had been stronger and cleverer than me. She was talking now about my illness, and what she knew about it, talking about it to those around her, while I was in my room, crying because I was totally unable to be in her place, unable to tell her that she shouldn't try to own my illness, or turn it into something to her advantage, or use it to evoke sympathy for me.

My body hurt, every part of me I could feel hurt, and fever was burning my eyes. And I was still worried that the sound of my crying might reach them outside the room. This made me feel more miserable, more tearful and more ill, while my chest went on burning with every cough, and my nose was drowning under all the tears. I passed on the task of breathing to my mouth so as not to choke. Then, as the tears started dropping into my mouth, they calmed me again, and their salty taste numbed me until I fell asleep.

I woke up shivering, then felt the dried-up tears cracking on my face. The illness had not left me, although three days had passed already. Usually people felt better on the third day.

Though I knew that I had no money in my wallet, and that I didn't have the strength for it at all, I had to go to get medicine. I had to find the energy.

After a few moments of silence, I heard my mother's voice behind the door. Although she was an evil woman, her mutterings at prayer time were like the shy, hesitant chirpings of a little bird. A shiver ran through my body again, spreading through every inch, to be followed by a choking sound from an Egyptian film or soap opera. I pulled my shivering body out of the bed, and walked to the door of the room. I pushed the handle downwards, and felt as though my hand was about to shatter. As soon as I had opened the door, a wave of clean, comforting warm air wrapped itself around my face like a piece of velvet.

My mother was reclining on one of the sofas, covering herself with a blanket. She must have felt warm underneath it. She didn't turn in my direction, despite the unmistakable sound of the door opening. I went over to her and asked her to give me some money. She turned towards me with a look of contempt and asked me what for. Was it, for example, because I'd been lazing about in bed all day and hadn't even gotten up to help her clean the house?

I tried not to leap over and strangle her, strangle all that pain she was creating in me. I didn't reply, but went straight out of the house.

Outside, it was cold, dark and wet. I looked at my father's parking place but it was empty. Had he come back and gone out again, or had he not returned since the morning?

I climbed the stairs leading to my brother's apartment, where he lived with his wife.

I looked at him. This was my brother, and not the slightest resemblance between us to evoke any sort of connection. I stood close to him, so close it was almost disturbing, without realizing why. I did realize why: I couldn't stand the false closeness between him and his wife, who was sitting opposite him on a separate sofa. When I asked him for money, he didn't reply and didn't look at me, though after a few moments he might have smiled scornfully.

I turned towards his wife, who had not taken her eyes off the television screen. How wrinkled her face had become. She didn't look at me either. Had my sickness made me invisible? Her eyes, which were glued to the same soap that was playing on the first floor, twinkled in the light radiating from the screen. Next to her, my brother hadn't changed much. Only the power that moved him had changed: once it had been my father, so he couldn't stand my mother; then it had been my mother, so he couldn't stand his wife; and now it was his wife, so he couldn't stand anyone. For the whole three days I had spent here, neither he nor his wife had set foot in my parents' house. Instead, when she wanted to see him, my mother had to climb the staircase to the third floor. All day long he lay on his back on the sofa, while she, his wife, sat on the sofa opposite. From time to time he would look at her, begging her acceptance, while she looked at him, begging his love. On one of my recent visits she had confided to me that he was cheating on her. He had confessed to her himself, after she had caught him talking to a girl on the telephone, and he had sworn that it would be the last time. Of course, she'd told me all this so that I would speak to him. I'd pretended I would help her, then dropped the subject, as I had no real relationship with my brother, other than that we both tried as hard as possible to bear the sight of each other, without real success.

He had never even been able to form a natural relationship with a woman. We all knew who had made him marry his wife. On the other hand, what did I know of that woman he loved, but couldn't manage to be with?

Oh brother.

What did I even know of my brother; who or what he was? Was he really my brother? What was there between us, apart from laughter that never came from the heart? How he had aged. And when would I find that I too had aged? That change that is slower than yesterday's day turning into night.

Finally he turned his eyes towards me, with a look of disgust, wondering how I could be so impertinent as to ask him for money. I knew my brother well, and was used to this look of his, which he would turn on anyone he was confident he could be frank with, a frankness that would unleash an enormous feeling of disgust inside him. After the look, he asked: "Do you know me? Do I know you?"

How I would have liked to know you, how I would have liked you to know me. But instead I answered him: "My ass." That was my answer to a question that was wrongly timed and had nothing to do with my request. Keep your money for yourself, and buy whatever bit of bad taste takes your wife's fancy.

Even his taste in clothes and his way of dressing had changed. His face above his shirt collar and his belly behind his buttons had changed, too. I hope you don't lose your hearing as well: the last thing left for you to connect to something different from this world of yours, so you can listen to your intellectual lover on the telephone without your wife finding out about that conversation.

I retraced my steps, forcing my way through the forest of unused furniture with which my sister-in-law had filled her world. My temperature had returned to burn my eyes again, as I looked in disbelief at the sheen on the apartment floor.

I woke to the sound of the door being opened. How long since I had last heard it. I kept my eyes closed to enjoy it until the end, and when I opened them, my sister appeared in front of me, holding her daughter in her left arm. I'd only woken once that night, I now recalled. She was smiling as her eyes took in the walls of the room, and I felt the blessing of someone visiting me.

Although my room was not large, it took her some time to get close to my bed. The breeze that had slipped in with her when she came into the room had beaten her to me, and revived me slightly. I pulled my body up a little and smiled. Still walking towards me, she said dispassionately in a nasal voice:

"Hello."

Then,

"How are things?" I didn't reply. It was quite obvious how things were. I stretched my hands out towards her daughter and was surprised when she didn't try to stop me, but I soon understood the reason, as the child turned her face away from me. Yes, turned her face away. "You see? She doesn't like you!" my sister remarked, as if she thought that such a comment wouldn't hurt.

Yes, I saw. She pushed my leg aside and sat on the edge of the bed, where she started to play with her child, who laughed solemnly. The whole scene unfolded as if I were not there, as if my right leg weren't touching her back. Then she went on and on talking into her daughter's little ears, absolute nonsense everything she was saying, she who had never been a talkative person. Then suddenly, as I watched them silently, I realized that my sister was merely trying to give her daughter all her love and to treat her as we'd one day dreamed, under the influence of the movies, of being treated ourselves. For no apparent reason, this saddened me.

She turned towards me and asked,

"What?"

I raised my eyebrows then lowered them again. She said that she'd called in the morning and my father had told her that I'd been ill for four days. I smiled, then replied: "Yes."

She asked me if I'd eaten anything and I said: "No."

She put her little girl down on the carpet and before leaving the room asked me not to harm her. Soon after, the child started to scream. I tried not to feel angry. She was looking straight at me, her eyes filled with tears and her tiny hands shaking in the air. I looked back at her calmly as she screamed on and on without taking her eyes off my face. I didn't know what she saw in me. Then my temperature started to go up again. I didn't need her to cry like this.

My sister came back with a piece of bread on a plate, a slice of cheese lying on top of it. The slice of cheese raised my fears regarding its expiration date, and I was sure that if it hadn't been for the child crying, I would have done much better. I had been hoping for soup, even powdered soup from a packet, as the worst of the likely options.

After she threw the plate in front of me, she bent over her daughter, looking at me with a faintly reproachful smile.

"What did you do to her, you little devil?"

So I smiled, too. "Nothing. I swear."

Her warm reproach brought my temperature down a little, its place again taken by a pleasant coolness, as usual accompanied by small drops of sweat. The two of them embraced each other. After a few moments, I became aware of a new image of my sister, which I had only now discovered: her breast in her baby's mouth. My sister had become a mother. Then I suddenly recalled something I hadn't fully understood when it happened. I was visiting her with my parents. There was one moment when my mother went to pick up the baby, which had started to cry, and my sister dashed over and snatched the baby away from her. The child fell asleep. My sister removed her nipple from her mouth, and the little one quivered like a sparrow, then carried on sleeping. As my sister very slowly started to button her blouse, I noticed some bruises on her breast. When I asked her about them, she replied that maybe she'd knocked against something, so I suggested that perhaps it was her husband who had knocked her. She said, in a quiet but very angry voice, that I shouldn't start my nonsense about her husband.

My sister had early on discovered that the most precious thing she had was her femininity. This was a sort of unlucky coincidence in our house, where femininity was a flaw. As a result, whatever she did, she found herself on the losing side. By contrast, of course, and in order to secure my freedom, I had since childhood always chosen the stronger side. All of us, my mother, father, brother, and myself, regarded her and her beauty with contempt. Sometimes we would fight her and punish her, as we, the thinking people, were concerned with the different forms of knowledge, and not with the trivialities of appearance. My sister, on the other hand, had been, and still was, both beautiful and provocative. Her breasts were much bigger than mine, and while she liked to show hers off, I would hide mine, not wishing to attract anyone's attention to this burgeoning disgrace that would lead me to the same fate as the condemned and the handicapped. I even succeeded in concealing my periods so well that five years after I had left home my mother actually asked me whether I was having them yet.

Then my sister's husband arrived, to continue the family saga by punishing her again, and for exactly the same reason: jealousy. His trump card was my sister's previous relationships, before she got to know him, that is. He himself had of course had several relationships, mostly paid for. Then just before getting married he had played his trump card and told her he would be unable to marry her because she wasn't a virgin, thereby enabling himself to enslave her and torture her without any objection on her part. Of course, he married her because she was from a rich family, or perhaps because she'd look pretty beside him, and his car, home, garden, and job.

I asked again, in a voice that I tried to make as unobtrusive and unthreatening as possible, about things between them, and whether they were getting any better now. She hesitated for a moment then said that she no longer cared. She was living with him in a purely materialistic relationship: he had a car that she could use whenever she wanted, a house and a garden, and he gave her money so she didn't need to work.

I asked her whether they had sex, she said yes, that was how they had had their little girl. He really hadn't wanted the child, and had tried to force her to have an abortion, threatening her with everything and eventually with divorce. But she had been ready, so she told me, to give up her marriage, her life, everything, but not the unborn child.

"You can't believe what happiness it is to have a child. I never thought of having a child before, but now I feel it's the most beautiful thing I've ever done and lived in my life."

There was enough weakness and misery in her voice for me to believe her completely, perhaps for the first time. She knew he was unfaithful to her. Every time before he went to his lover, he would make a huge scene to justify his lengthy absence afterwards. But what could she do, go back to living with my parents? Anything would be more bearable than living with them.

"Have you forgotten?"

I suddenly felt the tears rising to my throat. I almost choked as I tried not to cry, so I coughed and cried at the same time. "Cheers!" she said, and told me to stop crying, then tried to console me, saying that I was the happiest of the family, since at least I lived as I pleased.

Was it conceivable that anyone could envy the way I lived, with all my sadness, misery, and loneliness? I found myself telling her about the telephone conversation I'd heard a few days ago, and she asked me if I was an idiot.

My parents had been separated for more than two years, each one living in a separate room. My mother slept in her, my sister's, room, while my father slept in my brother's room, leaving their original bedroom to the darkness.

The Shahinaz affair was known to everyone. My mother had called her and told her of her own existence, then the two of them had in turn sat down with my father, and it was decided that he and my mother should separate. Forever. My mother wouldn't let my father touch her until the day she died, and he could go with any whore that took his fancy. It was decided that a special account should be opened for my mother, into which a specified sum would be transferred at the beginning of each month. In addition, my father would waive all his rights to the house. A deed of ownership was therefore drawn up in favor of my mother, who would be entitled to evict him if he brought any other woman to the house; until then he would be entitled to remain there, to prevent scandal and preserve the appearance of a united family despite everything.

And I, for two years, hadn't seen any of that. I hadn't even noticed that they had separated.

I awoke to the squirming of a crying child. I was alone in the room. I had slept for perhaps half an hour. I went out to the sitting room. My niece was on the sofa under the blankets, preparing herself for a major crying session. My sister's bag was beside her, while the house was clean and empty. I opened the purse and took some money, then went to the bathroom to urinate. My urine had a putrid smell, like tuna salad.

As I came back from the bathroom, the child in the sitting room had started to cry. I made my way to my own room, put the money in my wallet, and started to cry with her. I was tired as I'd never imagined it was possible to be tired, and scared as well. All I wanted was to hold the baby, but I couldn't even hug her, this only beautiful thing in my sister's life.

I went back to the sitting room, my bones shivering inside me. It was her daughter. Her tiny eyes were entirely covered by a film of tears, which overflowed and ran down to her ears as soon as she saw me. I stretched out my little finger and wiped the tears from her face. They were not warm, and I couldn't stop myself from touching her again. I would infect her, no doubt.

I left my right hand on her back, listening to the rhythm of her agitated body as it sighed, like an anguished soul, while my left hand bore all her weight. How frightening for such a fragile thing to be between my hands. I went on carrying her around the house.

"Sleep, my sweetheart."

We were telling each other.

My sister opened the door and said goodbye. When I told her that I'd taken some money from her wallet, she suddenly started talking in a humiliating way, which surprised me, about the money, and how it had been set aside to buy milk. The same old story as my mother's whenever I tried to beg for a little money that I didn't really need, except that I loved my mother's money.

I tried to ignore her, and thought she was just being obstinate. She asked me to give it back immediately, but I refused, and she said that was the last time I'd do that to her.

And the first.

She seemed really angry, while I carried on with my indifference. Then I saw her shout in my direction that I was cheap, then slam the door behind her, waking up her sleeping child, so that she started screaming again. I had to cry too. As if we could never bear the idea of love in this house.

I had cried enough. I masturbated to replenish my empty mind with fantasies. My smell couldn't be any worse now. A short while before, my mother had come into the room and thrown some money in front of me, saying that I must have been staying in bed all these days because I was angry that she hadn't given me money. Then she asked, only rhetorically, who I thought she was saving money for if not for me and my siblings. It wasn't a bad sum. I looked at it warily, uncertain whether to take it or rip it up. I was more inclined to take it. It couldn't be worse than what she thought of me already. Then I cried again. I cried a bit more than enough. It was time to leave. I put the money in my wallet behind the two notes that I'd taken from my sister, then stood up. For a moment I almost fainted, so I went back to bed.

Before I'd come to visit my family my wallet had been full of money, but I'd stocked up on fuel and bought presents for my brother and his wife, and for my mother and father, as well as my sister and her baby, so there wasn't a single *mallim* left with me. Once again, more precisely this time, I calculated how much I had lost as a result of this visit. Outside, beyond the door of my room, the delicate mathematical calculations I was performing coincided with the noise of rapid movements that did not fit my mother's rhythm. My father. I called out to him in a voice that was unfamiliar to me, perhaps because of the illness, perhaps because I hadn't used it for a long time, or perhaps for both reasons together.

"Father?"

"Yes."

It was my father. "I want some money," I said.

"Why?"

"I just do."

I summoned all my strength once again, grabbed a towel and left my room. The sitting room was empty apart from the noise of the flames in the fireplace. I went into the bathroom, turned on the tap above me, and had a long pee. From the other side of the bathroom door I heard my father's voice say, "I put the money beside your bed." Then I started to shower, regaining the feeling of my body under the sparkling elegance of the water.

While I was rubbing everything off my body, as I pulled the sponge over my left hand, I felt a light but enjoyable pain. That was what carrying my sister's baby the day before had left on my arm.

I now smelled clean. I would brush my teeth after I ate. I took the money from beside the bed. At least I hadn't lost out financially, there had even been a small profit. I got dressed and headed for the kitchen, but there was nothing in the disgusting enormous fridge. Only bread and yogurt. I took them out, went out onto the balcony and started to eat, keeping my eyes on the neighbors' closed windows, as I couldn't face the whiteness of the yogurt.

My brother had come a few minutes before, and sat down beside me without saying a word. He just took out a note and slipped it into my pocket. Him as well! He also tried to take the piece of bread away from me, but I quickly moved it away from him, so he burst out laughing, and I smiled at his stupidity, and for feeling sorry for him. Suddenly, as the sourness of the yogurt filled my mouth, I found myself asking him: "Do you know anyone called Shahinaz?"

He pretended to laugh again: "What, did you hear a quarrel between my parents?"

I pretended that that was it, and he added cynically: "My father's girlfriend."

"Girlfriend?"

He stood up and left the balcony for the garden, where he started to walk up and down on the lawn with his hands behind his back. From time to time the wind would race him, shaking the grass around him. He'd become really ugly, his body completed changed. As I finished my yogurt, I went on searching for something in him

125

that resembled my memory of what he had once been. Even his fingernails had changed.

I finished my yogurt, but a small piece of bread was left, so I crumbled it between my fingers and threw into the air for a passing bird. As I followed it upwards with my gaze, my eyes hurt the moment I saw the sky. I had forgotten how blue the sky could be!

I went in and threw the spoon into the sink. The sound of it falling was the last thing I heard in the house.

I hadn't noticed it getting dark, as if I had suddenly hit the darkness.

It had started raining again, so I drove carefully, happy that my wallet was swollen with money. As soon as I got there, I would go to a good restaurant. But when would I get there? The darkness around me was pitch black, and I didn't know how to occupy my mind to stay awake. All I could see was the black asphalt, lit up by the car's headlights as it sped along the highway; the wipers, monotonously wiping the shadows of the raindrops from the car's windshield; and my hands on the steering wheel. Watching the shadows, I forgot myself for a critical moment and my hands lost control of the steering wheel, but I managed to slam on the brakes at exactly the right time. I had almost died! After that, a wave of warmth spread through my body, weighing me down between the legs.

A feeling of peace returned, making me forget everything. Had it not been for the cold sweat on my face in the wake of the wave of warmth, I'd have forgotten I existed at all. After a while, I started to want to sleep but, afraid that I might actually do so, tried to convince myself in this dark void that I had to get there.

I got there. It was still raining, so I hurried inside. My single brief hesitation was in front of some almond blossom petals that had fallen by the restaurant door. I tried blowing on them but couldn't find enough breath to move them, even a little. Instead, I was overcome by a violent cough. I mustn't rush into an adventure like making almond blossoms flutter again.

The restaurant was almost empty, for it was a bit before supper time, and it was some time before I could order my meal. As I entered the staff were eating their supper. I could watch them eat in a mirror hanging on the wall. There were two girls among them, most likely the waitresses. The first one had her mouth extremely close to the plate and looked uncouth, and the second seemed to be dreaming rather than having her supper. When they had finished, one brought the menu and the other took my order: chicken soup and a glass of wine. She had a very strange body.

Some other people had just come in: three men, who sat down at the table next to mine. One of them, the best-looking one, proceeded to stare at me shamelessly. I looked at his reflection in the glass of the picture hanging on my right. Though the food was bad, I ate it all, purely out of habit, then ordered a second glass of wine to give myself the chance to look at the man for a little longer. A little wine had spilled onto the white paper napkin under the glass, so every time it was put back, it left a new mark. The sight of those marks gradually gave me a terrible feeling of loneliness.

I lifted my head in the man's direction so as to look straight at him, and found him looking at me, as if to say goodbye.

When I got up, I found that I needed to pee, so I asked for the bill and headed for the restroom to save time, which I didn't know what to do with anyway. The paper handkerchiefs in the lavatory were extra soft, so I took several and divided them between my various pockets. I find that I love clean paper handkerchiefs. When I returned, girl number two came up to me and told me that the gentleman (pointing to the handsome one) had paid my bill.

Alright.

I went up to him and thanked him. He put his hand out to shake mine, and invited me to sit down.

Italians. A doctor, a journalist, and a photographer. He was the journalist, unfortunately. The ugly photographer I found surprisingly charming, while the doctor was just ordinary, but my handsome friend was boring, like any young, ambitious journalist. We went on drinking and laughing, and so that the photographer wouldn't dream I might sleep with him, I kept eye contact with the journalist.

I stood up with a little difficulty, fully convinced that I wouldn't be able to drive the car, for there had been a powerful propaganda campaign to this effect. I said I'd walk, the photographer said he'd drive me, and the journalist said he'd drive me, while the doctor remained outside the discussion.

As we all emerged onto the damp street, it seemed the journalist was right. He drove, with me sitting quietly beside him. He asked me "Where to?" just once, and I told him. Before he should have turned left towards my house, he turned right, but I didn't care. He asked if I cared to ask him where he was taking me, and I said no.

We arrived at his house, and I followed him into the sitting room, then he went to the kitchen, and I followed him. He poured himself a vodka, then asked me whether I'd like one as well. We took our two glasses back to the sitting room. He sat there, with me beside him, my eyes glued to a map on the wall, while we sipped our drinks.

I woke up to find myself alone and naked in a bed that I did not recognize. I looked around and found my clothes neatly arranged, with my shoes beside them, and my socks lying on top of the shoes. There was nothing to suggest a rape scene. I tried to recall what had happened, but the only thing I could remember was the sound of a wrapper being torn open, like that of a packet of peppermint sweets. Most likely it was a condom packet.

As I was getting dressed and putting my shoes on, I looked at how neatly arranged the room was. There were two books on the windowsill, a small one on top of a bigger one, and beside them were some coins, also carefully arranged according to size. I stood in front of them, uncertain whether to take them or not.

Outside, it was still morning. I walked along the empty street, uncertain what time it was now. At last I spotted a young man in the distance, walking in my direction down the sidewalk. By the time I'd collected my thoughts, he'd already passed me, so I turned round to stop him and ask the time.

Just after half past nine.

My visits to my family were always full of surprises. I could never guess what would be waiting for me. The first day was nice; it hadn't yet started to rain, and we all had breakfast together in the garden.

Suddenly the clouds gave way to the morning light, which was too weak to dry my tears.

The End

At first, I tried subterfuge, making the narrator a woman, then a man. I also wanted to speak in the third person, masculine or feminine, so as to give an element of fiction to what is actually real, and that, in truth, this narrator is me.

Me.

The fact is that the only thing that still preoccupies and confuses me is food. What to eat and when? What are the benefits of each meal? How can I maintain a balance between the various vitamins I'm consuming? My physical health has become the most important thing in my life. My body is strong, and my bosom is tight and well rounded, so that when I tried on one of my friends' dresses in front of her, she even praised its mature and hard shape. When I wear tight trousers, my colleagues admire my bottom. My stomach is also getting almost completely flat. All this is because I eat sensibly and do various sports, as well as walking and swimming. I walk every day in beautiful natural settings to relax my nerves, which anyway never become tired. As I walk, I let my arms hang freely at my sides, so that the tension melts away from my neck area. My arms are normally crossed, even when I am sitting in bed dreaming. I try to persuade myself to let them hang free, but they seem not to know how to do anything except clasp one other, one on top of the other. For my part, I usually surrender to their obstinacy and try to relax, accompanied by their unexplained spasms.

At other times, suddenly, and for no obvious reason, as I indulge myself in one of my activities of rest and recuperation, my eyes fill with tears. Crying is not a useful activity, I presume, but I find it to be the thing that, after eating, most agrees with my style of life, for my spirit is completely ruined. Without any particular effort, I find myself thinking of death while I shop for food that has not been genetically modified or treated with chemicals. Not just then, but all the time. When someone sits down in front of me and begins to talk in an ordinary way about a plan for a period six months hence, and then, after a few sentences, talks about a plan for two years later, I find myself lost in admiration for him. I am not even sure I'll be alive next month, now that the idea of suicide has become the most serious of my projects. This idea, though, has not kept me from continuing to take care of my health. But the thought of health has also not prevented the thought of death. Nothing could prevent the thought of death. Those periods of time, six months or two years, that some people start to plan for as though this were so straightforward, have always seemed to me like an enormous expanse of nothingness. My whole life is shrinking, on its way to disappearance. I spend my day alone in bed, scarcely moving and thinking of nothing but death. Or becoming a different person, for the me that is now me is diseased and has become unbearable. I cannot stand anything that it does or feels. I cannot stand its way of seeing and thinking: its conversation, its exhibitionism, its stupidity, its boring taste, its feeling of cold. The same feeling of cold runs through my body. True, I have moved to a new city and a new house but my inner self has stayed the same. The furniture arrangement in my new house bears the marks of my taste, which it serves up to me daily in a perfectly monotonous way. My bed; my work table; the little shelf of books whose vertical titles I look at with a complete lack of self-control, rereading their titles from my bed so many times that my eyes become my prison. The same titles for such a long time, and my life has become exactly like them; like the pictures hanging on the wall. They all stay the same, for the first day is the same as today, and the same as tomorrow. The same sideways glance from Su'ad Husni to Muharram Fu'ad; the same hunter from the Shahnameh, and the same gazelles in the field. And the flute in the mouth of the musician that emits no sound. The same silence.

I realize quite well that sometimes a small nod of the head is sufficient for someone to discover some beauty that he can clutch at, and so keep him alive a little longer. Yet I also realize that my own such nods have grown rare, not just because of my attentiveness to the potential damage to my back, but also because I have no more room for improvisation, apart from that dictated by my physical exercises or the spasms that my body has to endure much of the time. Rather, the obsessed realm that I have gradually and naturally come to live in has transformed me into an egotistical being, driven to sleep alone every night, far from anyone's touch. No one touches me. No one will touch me. I will not let anyone touch me.

I stand on the edge of the swimming pool, on the diving board, among all the exposed bodies, and my sense of horror only increases. I look for some strength that will impel me to share this same water that has touched their skin, to walk on streets where my shoes will pick up all the dirt of the universe. I stroll in a public park where different people walk, with different shapes and voices and different interests, but only one sensation fills me. A girl is talking on the phone, and her voice kills me. Time after time I try to ignore it, then I try to follow what she is saying, but I know that I hate her and probably wish she were dead. Another man is walking with a stick. He has a broken leg. He takes advantage of this so that a second girl lets him sit down on the bench beside her. Then he starts talking to her in a voice so soft as to be annoying; she maybe doesn't reply, and I don't know why she doesn't get rid of him.

There are always people, coming and going all the time. They are all talking. Talking, either in a whisper or in loud voices, around me. Despite their differences, they are all similar: ugly and horrible. They come and go all day looking for love. Alone, yes, like me. But I hate them all. And I am sure other people hate them, too. Other people who know them well, while I feel their reasons for hating them, and that these reasons are real and convincing. When someone talks to me about someone else, I can only think of things to arouse hatred of that person, and the person in front of me will agree with everything I say. And if the second person were before me, I would give him at least as many reasons to hate the first person. Yes, there are all the reasons to hate, and I can see nothing else. I can hate the whole world, and for good reasons, whose validity is not in doubt. As a consequence, it has become difficult for me to respect anyone; respect requires a great effort on my part. But even if, even if, I am sometimes nice to people, and as a result joy overtakes me, this springs merely from a wish to show them they are not nice. And so I make them feel the same alienation and pain as I do.

I don't deny that the only places I have come to feel comfortable are deserted ones. Anywhere that other people have deserted; anywhere that scares them off. There, I no longer feel the burden of hatred, but only myself; the self that will never love, but only feign love, then leap in the other direction and ask: "Do you see, I was right from the beginning?" Right to hate my family, neighbors, and friends. Right to work for nothing except to stir up hatred, the only thing that still gives me the energy to act. I run around among people for no other purpose than to give them every justification and excuse to hate. Yes, I have become capable of the worst, and how easy and true that is, at the end of the day. In a quite natural and familiar manner, I have come to prefer that everyone should die and the air be soft and spring-like forever.

How have I reached this point, where I can no longer see anything except for the evil that surrounds my eyes? Why is it that everything that was as it should be, no longer is? My face is contracted. My lips force themselves up towards my nose, and at the point where they meet, over my front teeth, I feel hatred form, well up, then proceed to destroy me. My nerves are destroyed, and soon I am on the verge of tears. Fragile, like straw. I can no longer move my athletic body from where it lies in bed, once again discovering that it is just a collection of gray cells, part of the darkness of this clean and tidy house. Then it is struck with terror as it suddenly realizes the consequence of total hatred. The silence of the telephone. The absence of people knocking on the door. The stillness. The certain knowledge that no one will lie beside me.

In fact, I can no longer receive anyone at my house. Whoever the man is, he will tread on the carpet and ruin it. If he makes coffee the next morning, he will pour yesterday's grounds down the kitchen sink. I'll come in feeling anxious, but have to put on a brave face when I find him standing by the stove waiting for the water to boil, coffee grounds coating the sink. Then he'll use the bathroom. That, and the remains of his dry sperm on my legs, will disgust me. Wow. That thing, sex; I can't believe that I was once able to do it and even enjoy someone touching me. How did I dare, how did I let anyone touch me? No. No. Sexually transmitted diseases have come to make me very worried. I would prefer to have sex using a condom, and when the man with me reaches orgasm, to tie up the condom with his sperm in it and give it to him before sending him on his way; then go back home, clean up, and drink my coffee by myself. But that would be difficult. I know I'd like to do it, but what sort of person would I be afterwards?

Rather, who would want to stay with an outcast like me? I, who am beyond the limit. I, who can't help but lead a man to his furthest limits, this being the most persistent and longest-lasting of all my traits. I could have led hundreds down this path of mine to the edge. But everyone has left me, and now here I am alone, a lonesome shepherdess, who can do nothing to perfection except find pleasure in calmly hating. For many years I have tried to behave differently, to love and to give, to open up and let my carpets acquire wrinkles. But besides a little local happiness, I would also feel a torrent of insincerity and sadness. Perhaps it is all because I was not raised on the principles of love, but of distance and loneliness. And ever since A died I have concluded that I will never change. I am not going to become a better person. I lack the love to become a better person. I lack love. I lack love terribly. Or perhaps I lack the strength to pretend to love, to do that well, and my last chance was A. A.

When A suddenly became ill, he suddenly became my best friend. We had known each other before, but after finding out that he was ill I started to visit him regularly. As if I had suddenly discovered he was alive. I would visit him once every three days in the hospital where he was dying. The first time I visited him, he remembered me only with difficulty, but I helped him, and he was nice to me. There were a lot of other people visiting him who had also discovered the pleasure of attending to someone on his death bed. Which can indeed bestow some humanity on a person who wakes up one day and feels he is lacking a lot of it. Because I am an obsessive person, I made more of these visits, and I started to bring him lots of presents—things like flowers, books, and chocolate, for I was not yet aware of the harm this type of food can do. I would buy him all these things when I didn't have enough money to buy food for myself. Yes, I was never able to perfect any sense of balance. Instead, I would go to friends and eat at their houses, and they all came to the same conclusion about me: that I was an exploitative person who would visit them just so as to eat.

But as time went on, A, despite being on his death bed, became unable to stand me, for he still retained a modicum of sense. I began to sense that I was imposing myself on the last few moments of his life, which he might prefer to be spending alone. One day, things came to a head. It was lunch time, and one of the nurses brought him some soup. Tomato broth, with some cheap vegetables like potatoes and onions in it. A said that he didn't like this sort of food, and couldn't chew anything anymore, even though he was hungry. I tried to persuade him to eat a little of it. He wasn't entirely persuaded, but I didn't wait for him to be. I raised his bed and started to feed him, one spoonful after the other. At first he tried to refuse, but I insisted on forcing the spoon into his mouth. After several spoonfuls, when the tomato broth had started to run from his mouth onto his chin and then his clothes, he said in an angry, almost tearful, voice that he didn't want to eat. It was only then that I realized he really didn't want to eat. Three days later, I was planning on visiting him again, not caring what he had come to feel about me, when someone informed me that he had died. The only effect this information had on me was to make me cross his name out in my notebook and remove it from my extremely full schedule for the day. I felt I'd gained two hours of free time and a less stressful day. And no, I didn't go to his funeral, funerals being a type of collective activity in which the participants share the fruits of the importance death bestows on life. I have never been ready to share this with anyone; I have wanted it, this importance, for myself alone, again without obvious reason.

All this only shows that I am lacking love. Definitely. But I have come to live the opposite, and be the worst person of all: the most awkward, the most lacking in feeling. I have come to feel each minute pass as if it is against me. I go into a café to drink a fresh fruit juice, and because it takes the waitress several minutes to come to my table, I start wondering whether they hate me in this café, whether they don't want me there at all, because I am an intolerable person. A long time passes in fear and terror. Everything every moment is in terror of hatred. For I see how everyone hates me. So I had to move where no one knew me, and where I could try to love once again. But after a short time I would forget myself and be filled with hatred again, then chide myself and torture myself for what I am feeling: that I prefer a place full of hatred. Or perhaps the place where I am is already like this, but fails to acknowledge it. For hatred to achieve sincerity and depth without the need to hide itself anymore; for us to surrender to it without hesitation, and without denial, so that the face may be at rest and no longer contracted. How nice a feeling! In this place, I wouldn't have to bother about anything anymore, and nothing would bother me. Neither the engines of destruction nor the hammers of the builder. Harmony would return to the universe. The ugly would sit beside the deserted, without bringing sorrow to anyone's heart. No longer would the rough cloth of a coat cause anyone pain. From now on I will despise my coat, for I am untroubled by the cold, dry wind from which it tries to shield me. No, I will give in to the wind, I will leave it to dry my lips until they split, and a little blood will flow, then dry, then flow again, to remind me of the little pain that can kill me. No, I am no longer tempted either by the cure, or by the hopes of it. I wake up every day filled with resignation, feeling at peace to have arrived here, where love is no longer my only concern. I no longer care about it, or about anyone, or about any of the memories that remind me that at one time everything was all right, but no longer. No longer can I make myself avoid my true nature and my capacity for destruction, nor the death that dwells within me, and into which I have wanted to drag everyone, to where lie the true shadow and blackness of the self. The fact that we are truly and simply sordid. This is the truth. Even my friends' child waits for me to disappear in the darkness of the house's narrow staircase, then angrily but insistently screams, "I don't love her." I didn't turn my head to look back, I didn't have the courage, I just continued on my way. It was already too late. And only because of the several glasses of wine that I'd drunk before that moment, I felt that the darkness of the stairwell was getting more vicious. Even children? It was another two steps before the voice of her father could be heard in the playroom, saying, "You mustn't say that, sweetheart." Yes, perhaps one shouldn't say that, but that doesn't contradict the fact that even a child who only turned three five months ago doesn't love me anymore. Just like everyone else. No one wants to see me. Instead: to become someone that no one knows anything about. No one knows that it's started raining outside and that I don't have an umbrella or any warm clothes, but the pain in my heart is growing worse, and my body yearns to be buried, perhaps in that small little graveyard that I looked at peacefully while on my way to my friends' house. But before the tears that welled up in the stairwell ran out of patience, I left. From the garden path I heard again her warm, childish laughter. No, it wasn't in her nature to hate anyone, my friends' child. And I could die. I could no longer stay in the same place. So I went very far away, without confessing to myself the real reason, for it was so painful, yet at the same time so trivial. But the truth didn't need me to confirm it. To confess that I let a child's burblings manipulate me so harshly as to push me around and make me wallow in my tears for several months. I go on hiding myself away, frightened by her hatred of me. Nothing moves me any longer except for that hateful limit—the inability to endure any more. When no one can stand me any longer and I cannot stand anyone any longer. The limit of hatred. Only then do I loosen my fingers and let go of everything I have held onto so desperately until that moment. I lie on my back in bed, as the days pass, my only worry being what that black spot on the ceiling might be. Could it be an insect, a worm, a mark from an old nail, paint from the wall flaking off? I no longer have the strength to go out into a world any larger than this spot, where I would have to wander alone, then go into a café alone, and there try hard to finish the drink I ordered with words that emerged from my mouth confused and garbled, after people going in and out, and the passers-by on the sidewalk, had discovered the truth about me. That I am a hateful person, sitting in a café, accompanied by my wretched vulnerability.

But suddenly, and without my knowing how, there stirs within me again a tiny measure that smells faintly of love. Warily, I start to walk amongst it, like walking through pain, delicately, not wanting to wake it. Then it disappears again, before I can even realize what this awakening of love has meant: its taste has already left me, like the almond blossom petals that stay so briefly on the branches. Thus everything becomes equal again in the darkness of existence, where only pain grows, and my own distance from love.

Translator's note

Adania Shibli's second novel, *We Are All Equally Far from Love*, was originally published in Arabic as *Kulluna Ba'id bi-Dhat al-Miqdar 'an al-Hubb* by al-Adab in 2004. Readers with access to the Arabic original will note that the six letters referred to on p. 25 of the English translation have been omitted from the English version at the request of the author. A small number of other minor changes have also been made to the text by the author during the translation process, with the result that in a few places the English version is no longer a strict translation of the original.

A short section of the novel was used as a "set text" at the Arabic/English translation workshop organized by the British Council in Cairo in January 2010, and the results of that exercise have been incorporated, with some modifications, into the text of the present translation. Thanks are due to all the workshop participants for their contributions to an argumentative, but nonetheless rewarding, week. The event would have been even more rewarding had not Adania Shibli herself, who was due to attend the event, been detained overnight by the authorities at Cairo Airport, and sent back the following day to where she had come from—a timely reminder that literature and politics in the Middle East are seldom very far apart.

In making this translation, I am grateful for the support and patience of all at Clockroot Books, particularly Hilary Plum, who edited the text, and Pam Thompson; and to Adania Shibli herself, who read the translation and saved me from several errors, as well as making a large number of suggestions for improvements.

Paul Starkey
Durham, England
September 2011